As Elaine came out of her room she bumped straight into Calum.

For a moment  . He was halfway th

'Oh!' Elaine pu   rself and found them pressed against a broad, naked chest.

Calum pulled the shirt over his head. His skin was hot under her hands. His shoulders were broad, powerful and well-proportioned. Seeing him in his businesslike dark suits, one would never have guessed that his body could be so beautiful.

'Elaine! I'm so sorry. Did I hurt you?'

She blinked and stepped back. 'No. It was—it was my fault. Excuse me.' She hurriedly stepped past him and went on her way.

Dear Reader

The wild and primitive scenery of the Douro valley. The white baroque palaces. What men would live and rule here? Calum came first, a tall and golden god, but then Francesca pushed her way into my mind. Then Chris, very much a man of the world. A family, then—outwardly tamed, but with hidden emotions as deep and hot-blooded as the land they lived in. Three cousins who filled my imagination, fascinating, absorbing, clamouring to come alive. And three wishes that had to come true. Then I thought of an anniversary, and saw a girl, sitting entirely alone on the riverbank...

Sally Wentworth

Sally Wentworth was born and raised in Herfordshire, where she still lives, and started writing after attending an evening class course. She is married and has one son. There is always a novel on the bedside table, but she also does craftwork, plays bridge, and is the president of a National Trust group. They go to the ballet and theatre regularly and to open-air concerts in the summer. Sometimes she doesn't know how she finds time to write!

Recent titles by the same author:

TO HAVE AND TO HOLD
ONE NIGHT OF LOVE
CHRIS
FRANCESCA

CALUM

BY
SALLY WENTWORTH

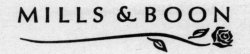

MILLS & BOON

MILLS & BOON and the Rose Device
are trademarks of the publisher.
Harlequin Mills & Boon Limited,
Eton House, 18-24 Paradise Road, Richmond, Surrey TW9 1SR
This edition published by arrangement with
Harlequin Enterprises B.V.

© Sally Wentworth 1995

ISBN 0 263 79265 X

Set in Times Roman 10 on 11½ pt.
07-9511-56450 C1

Made and printed in Great Britain

PROLOGUE

BRODEY HOUSE BICENTENNIAL

The magnificent eighteenth-century baroque palace of the Brodey family, situated on the banks of the River Douro in Portugal, will soon be *en fête* for a whole week to celebrate the two hundredth anniversary of their company.

The House of Brodey, famous the world over for its fine wines, especially port and Madeira, has now diversified into many other commodities and is one of the biggest family-owned companies in Europe. Originally founded in the beautiful island of Madeira, the company spread to Oporto when Calum Lennox Brodey the first went there two centuries ago to purchase thousands of acres of land in the picturesque Douro valley. That land is now covered with the millions of grape-vines that produce the port on which the family fortune is based.

A FAMILY AFFAIR

Just like any family, every member of the Brodey clan will be in Oporto to welcome their guests from all over the world to the festivities.

Patriarch of the family, Calum Lennox Brodey, named after his ancestor, as are all the eldest sons in the main line, is reported to be greatly looking forward not only to the celebrations but also to the family reunion. Old Calum, as he's popularly known in wine-growing circles, is in his eighties now but still takes a keen interest in the wine-producing side of the company, and is often to be seen by his admiring workers strolling among the vines to check on the crop or tasting the vintage in the family's bottling plant near Oporto.

STILL HAUNTED BY THE PAST

Although the anniversary will be a happy one, in the past there has been terrible tragedy within the family. Some twenty-two years ago Old Calum's two eldest sons and their wives were involved in a fatal car-smash while on holiday in Spain, all four being killed. Each couple had a son of roughly the same age and Old Calum bravely overcame his grief as he took the boys into his palace and brought them up himself, both of them eventually following in his footsteps by joining the company.

It was rumoured at the time of this overwhelmingly tragic accident that old Mr Brodey looked to his third son, Paul, to help run the business. Paul Brodey, however, was hooked on painting and is now a cel-

ebrated artist. He lives near Lisbon with his wife Maria, who is half Portuguese and is herself a well-known painter. The good news is, though, that their only child, Christopher, has joined the family firm on the sales side and is based mainly in New York.

Only one of Old Calum's grandsons now shares the splendour of the palace, which is mainly decorated in Renaissance style, with him. This is the only child of his late eldest son, who, following the family tradition, is also called Calum—Young Calum, in this case. The younger Calum Brodey, around thirty years old and one of the most eligible bachelors in the country, if not in Europe, has virtually taken over the running of the company, but will be gracefully taking a back seat to his grandfather during the week's festivities.

MARRIAGE IN MIND?

Another extraordinary tradition peculiar to the family is that all the men maintain their links with their mother country by marrying blonde English girls. Every son of the family for the past several generations has travelled to the UK and returned with a beautiful 'English rose' on his arm. Will Young Calum and Christopher carry on the tradition, we wonder?

The third Brodey grandson, Lennox, who now lives in Madeira with his beautiful and adored wife Stella, who is expecting their first child later this year, will be among the family guests. Stella, of course, is a blonde and lovely English girl.

Old Calum's fourth child, his elegant daughter Adele, is married to the well-known French millionaire, the gallant and still handsome Guy de Charenton, an assiduous worker for the Paris Opera and for the many charities that he supports.

Although the Brodey family has many connections with the upper echelons of society, especially in England, it was Adele's daughter and only child, the sensationally beautiful Francesca, who finally linked it to the aristocracy with her marriage to Prince Paolo de Vieira a few years ago. This marriage, which took place in the Prince's fairy-tale castle in Italy, looked all set to have the proverbial happy ending, but, alas, this wasn't to be and the couple parted after only two years. Since then Francesca's name has been linked with several men, including lately Michel, the Comte de la Fontaine, seen with her on her many shopping trips in Paris and Rome.

To all the glamorous members of the Brodey family we extend our warm congratulations on their anniversary, and we are sure that all their lucky guests will have the most lavish and memorable time at the bicentennial celebrations.

THE HOUSE OF BRODEY

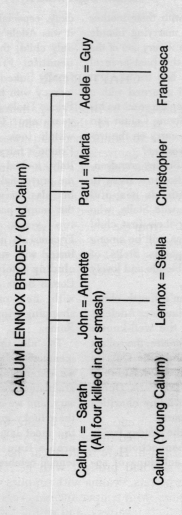

CALUM LENNOX BRODEY (Old Calum)

Calum = Sarah   John = Annette   Paul = Maria   Adele = Guy
(All four killed in car smash)

Calum (Young Calum)   Lennox = Stella   Christopher   Francesca

CHAPTER ONE

THEY were all there—the Brodeys—gathered together in the beautiful gardens of their magnificent baroque *palácio* near Oporto. All of them had come to celebrate the two hundredth anniversary of the House of Brodey.

Celebrating with them were a hundred and fifty or so guests, standing in groups around the lawn, drinking aperitifs before lunch was served, talking, laughing. The spring sky was an unclouded blue; there was just the faintest breeze from the nearby coast. The gardens were looking beautiful, carefully tended and full of flowers: a perfect day and a perfect setting. For the guests the lunch party was pure pleasure. For Elaine Beresford it meant work.

She stood as unobtrusively as possible in the background, making sure that the waiters were going to every group with their trays of drinks, that no one was left out. In the far garden the tables were already set for the exact number of guests who had accepted invitations. They would make their way to the tables in another half-hour or so, then she would have to oversee the serving of the food and wine, the clearing, and so on to the next course. A difficult enough task in England where she had staff that she hired frequently and knew and trusted, who spoke English. Here in Portugal she, and the two senior staff she had brought with her, had to cope through interpreters, dealing with supplies which hadn't arrived on time, with temperamental chefs who wanted to do things their own way, and with a thousand other things which could, and usually had, gone wrong.

9

And mostly, of course, she'd had to cope with the Brodeys.

Things were running smoothly at the moment and she was able to watch them as they moved among their guests. They were something else, the Brodey family. The first of them she'd met had of course been Francesca, or the Princess de Vieira, to give her full title. They had known each other in London, before Francesca had married her Italian prince, and when Elaine, too, was married. Now neither of them was. Francesca's marriage had ended in an ugly divorce, Elaine's in the plane crash that had killed Neil, her husband, three years ago. They had become unlikely friends, the jet-set lifestyle that Francesca lived a million miles away from Elaine's quiet country life. But after Neil had died, leaving little money, she'd turned a hobby into a business and started catering for weddings and parties. Francesca had asked her to organise her own wedding and that in turn had led to a whole lot more commissions and eventually to Elaine's organising and catering for this whole week of celebrations that the House of Brodey had laid on to mark their bicentennial.

Elaine had seriously considered refusing the commission; there were so many difficulties involved, not least the language. But she was ambitious for her company, wanted to see it grow, and, when it came down to it, she was unable to resist the simple challenge of seeing if she could do the job successfully.

Francesca's grandfather, old Mr Brodey, who was in his eighties, was the nominal head of the family and had taken a keen interest in the arrangements. But it had been to his grandson, the one they called Young Calum, that Elaine had sent her estimates and plans, had had long discussions with on the phone and pages of correspondence via the fax machine. Calum and Francesca were cousins; Elaine could see them both as they moved among their guests. Francesca was tall and beautiful in a brilliantly coloured outfit, Calum Brodey taller still, dwarfing most of the people there; both of them were fair-haired and English-looking among so many Portuguese. Francesca had a man in tow, some French count, but then, when didn't she have a man around?

Calum, it seemed, wasn't married, although he must be over thirty, Elaine guessed, and was very good-looking, in a hard, arrogant kind of way. She moved to direct a waiter towards a group with empty glasses, passing the circle round Calum as she did so. He was speaking to the guests in fluent Portuguese. Resuming her post on the steps leading to a door of the house where she could see easily, Elaine thought how strange it was to find this family who had been living and working in Portugal for the last two hundred years and yet still seemed so very English. They all spoke English as naturally and fluently as she did; their children were sent to England to school, and they all seemed to have married English people. Especially each heir: there was some strange kind of tradition that he should always marry an English blonde, so Francesca had told her.

There were few blondes here today; she could see only half a dozen among the women. And there was certainly no one with auburn hair like her own.

Glancing at her large-faced, practical watch, Elaine saw that it was close to the time they had arranged for the guests to go in to lunch. Again she approached the circle round Calum. Someone made way for her, thinking she was a guest, and she was able to say, 'I think it's time.'

'Of course.' Calum spoke to those near him, while Elaine moved to another group, saying her carefully rehearsed, '*Por favor, senhor, senhora. Almoço,*' and gesturing towards the other garden. It was more difficult because she spoke some Spanish and tended to use that accent instead of Portuguese. So she added, 'Lunch is being served,' for those who could speak English.

There was an awkward moment when it was found that there was one too many guests and an extra place had to be hurriedly laid, but the little incident was soon forgotten as the first course was served and wine was poured. Elaine kept in the background as much as possible, making sure that all was well in the kitchen as well as in the garden, trying to be in two places at once and succeeding well enough. She'd had enough experience of catering for buffet parties to know how much food to provide, which dishes would be the most popular, which centre-pieces would attract the most comment. Today she had chosen, after consultation with Francesca and Calum, a large model of the Brodeys' *barco rabelo*, a boat that was moored on the nearby River Douro, and which had once, long ago, carried the barrels of wine down from the vineyards further up the valley to their wine-lodge in Oporto.

The guests exclaimed at the boat, set on a bed of blue flowers to represent the river, with its sail emblazoned with the single word 'BRODEY'. It was a name that signified the pride of the company and that of the family which bore it. And they were a proud lot; Elaine had soon found that out. Especially Calum. She had suggested one or two ways they could cut the costs of the celebrations, ways that many of her customers had been happy to accept, but Calum had vetoed the suggestion with a brusque refusal: only the best was good enough for the Brodey company's guests.

The rest of the meal passed without incident, and afterwards Elaine was able to escape to the cloakroom for a few minutes. While she was there another girl came in, petite and blonde, one of the people who had been talking to the Brodey cousins before lunch, Elaine remembered.

Back outside in the garden, a post-prandial glass of port was being offered. Some of the guests had already gone, but there were still quite a few enjoying this last drink. Suddenly there was a sharp cry and the distinct sound of someone's face being slapped. An astonished silence fell as everyone looked in that direction. Elaine started to hurry over, but saw with relief that no waiter was involved. It appeared that the blonde girl she'd seen in the cloakroom just a few minutes ago had taken exception to something one of the other guests had said. Chris Brodey had already taken the man's arm and was escorting him out of the garden. Calum, too late, was standing in front of the girl protectively. Then Francesca went over and took the girl inside the house.

There had been a fascinated silence as everyone watched what was happening, but then people began talking again, many of the men giving rueful smiles and shrugging, evidently thinking it could have happened to anyone. Old Mr Brodey had been inside the house when it happened, but he came into the garden now, looked round and, seeing Elaine, beckoned her over. She started towards him but Calum came swiftly to her side and murmured, 'Please don't tell my grandfather what happened just now. I'll explain later.'

Elaine gave him a surprised look, but nodded and walked over to the old man. Anyone seeing her might easily have mistaken her for one of the guests, come over from England for the party perhaps. She was wearing a well-cut but simple and practical suit, a silk shirt and low-heeled shoes, but there was something about her slim figure, her carriage and the way she walked that suggested good breeding and gracefulness of manner.

Although she never pushed herself forward, she had an air of class and quiet dignity that made her stand out in any circle. Anyone seeing her at this party would immediately think that she came from a background of wealth and position.

It was partly true: she had been well-educated and did come from such a background, but it wasn't *her* wealth, *her* position. Her father had been the youngest son of rather staid parents—a rebel who had loved life and lived it to the full, usually in direct opposition to his parents. He had met Elaine's mother, an aspiring actress, while he was at college, and only a hasty marriage, again against his parents' wishes, had made Elaine legitimate. He had been killed in an accident not long afterwards, and her mother, who had no money of her own, had appealed to his parents for help. It was they who had paid for Elaine's education at a good school, who had let her visit them for several holidays. They had given her what they felt duty-bound to give, but no more, because they had always disapproved of her mother, who never rose above bit parts and commercials.

Old Mr Brodey gave her a smile of welcome as she walked up to him. 'The party went off exceedingly well, my dear. You're to be congratulated.' He spoke with warm kindness, a man who knew how to treat the people who worked for him, in whatever capacity. He was a charming old man, one it was impossible not to like, not to warm to, but Elaine guessed that he could also be ruthless if necessary—how else could he have held together and widely expanded what had been just a wine company into the large business empire it had become?

They talked for a few minutes, but then the last of the guests came up to say goodbye, and afterwards Calum came over and urged the old man to go up to his room to rest. When his grandfather had gone, protesting only a little, Calum said, 'I'm sorry I had to warn you, but I didn't want Grandfather troubled. He hasn't been too well lately.'

'Of course. I quite understand.'

He nodded and walked away. Elaine watched his tall figure, wondering if he was worried about taking over as head of the Brodey empire. Some men might have been, but somehow she couldn't see Calum being at all anxious; he seemed perfectly capable of doing anything he set his mind to, and doing it with imaginative, ambitious efficiency. And the ruthlessness that she suspected in his grandfather? Yes, she rather thought he had that too.

After the lunch, Elaine checked that everything had been cleared in the kitchen and that it had been left pristine clean, that the hired staff had been paid and the left-over food and opened bottles of wine distributed between them. Only then did she relax and go to her room.

It had been arranged that she should stay in the *palácio* while she was in Portugal, and had been given a pleasant room in a side-wing which overlooked a courtyard. One that had probably been used in former times by the upper-class servant of an upper-class guest, Elaine had thought with amusement when she was shown into it for the first time. It had no air-conditioning or heating, but there were shutters which could be closed to keep it cool in the summer and a fireplace for the winter, beneath one of the many pepper-pot chimneys which adorned the roof. It had a modern single bed and furniture, a hand-basin and a built-in shower, and was adequate for someone in her position, she supposed.

The two staff members she had brought over with her, both men, one a chef, the other an ex-head waiter, had been given similar rooms, and were having a siesta after their hard work that morning. Grateful to relax for a while, Elaine showered and changed into a casual skirt and shirt, then took a chair into the courtyard to sit and read in the sun for a while. She didn't see any members of the family again until the internal phone in her room rang and Calum asked to see her.

She found him in his study—a large businesslike room fitted up with all the latest communications technology. A room which he had put at her disposal and where she kept all the paperwork to do with this week. He was leaning back against his desk and gave her a rueful smile. 'I'm afraid there will be an extra guest for dinner tonight. I hope it doesn't throw you out too much.'

'Not at all.' She went over to the small desk he had put in the room for her and took out the file for the family dinner that evening. 'Is the extra guest male or female?'

'Female.' He came to stand beside her and look at the seating plan. 'Now, where shall we put her?'

She was aware of his closeness, aware of his strong masculinity, but pushed it out of her consciousness, as she had trained herself to do over the last three years.

'Here, I suppose, at the end of the table. Near Chris.' He pointed with a long, well-manicured finger. 'It's the young woman who was involved in that incident earlier,' he explained. 'Francesca—we—have invited her to dinner.'

'What's her name? I shall have to do a place-card for her.'

'Tiffany Dean.'

Elaine made a note of the name, then went over to the desk to write out a card in her elegant script, learnt specially for this kind of job at calligraphy classes. She expected Calum to leave, but he went back to stand at his own, very large desk and picked up some messages that had come in over the fax. When he'd looked at them, he said, 'The lunch went well, except for there being one too few places.'

Elaine felt like telling him she strongly suspected that there had been one too many guests, but refrained from doing so. It was the smallest thing and not worth arguing about, although she rather resented having her efficiency rebuked. But she remembered the traders' maxim—that the customer was always right—even though on this occasion she knew darn well that the customer was wrong.

'The party at your vineyard——' she began.

'The *quinta*.' He gave it the Portuguese translation.

'Yes. Do you have any more information on the numbers for me?'

'I haven't, but I expect Francesca may have.' He smiled at her. 'Let's go and ask her, shall we?'

She walked beside him through the cool corridors of the house, not quite sure yet which room was which, which door led where. They came to the big sitting-room that all the family seemed to use more than any other, but Francesca wasn't there, or out on the terrace that overlooked the garden.

'Let's have a drink while we wait for her, shall we?'

Calum went inside and she sat at the table on the terrace, watching him through the open doors as he expertly opened a bottle of sparkling wine. He was, she realised, a very attractive man—not only to women, because of his handsomeness, but in the way that he drew people's eyes, their attention. His arrogance should have been off-putting, could quite easily have created a barrier between himself and those he wasn't close to, but he also had charming manners and a friendly smile which dispelled the hardness. This afternoon she had seen both men and women eager to meet and talk with him, not just because he was the heir to the Brodey Corporation, but because it was a pleasure to do so. Her eyes still contemplating him, Elaine wondered why he wasn't married, and whether the social face that he showed to the world was his true personality.

He turned with the glasses of wine in his hands and caught her gazing at him. His left eyebrow rose slightly. Embarrassed at being caught, she flushed a little, then was angry with herself for doing so.

'Your gardens are beautiful,' she said hastily as he came out to join her.

'They're my grandfather's pride and joy.'

'But not yours?'

Calum gave a small shrug. 'I take an interest in them, of course, and I like to see them looking at their best, as they are now, but I'm afraid I'm not very knowledgeable on the subject. How about you?'

'I did get keen for a few years,' Elaine admitted, glad that the topic gave her an excuse to look out over the gardens. 'But then I moved into a flat that doesn't have a garden. I tried window-boxes but I'm away such a lot that even those got neglected, I'm afraid.'

'Does your work take you away a lot, then?'

'Yes, I do seem to be travelling more as the business expands, but mostly in Britain, of course; we've only recently started working in Europe.'

His had been a polite, conversational kind of question and her reply had been on the same lines, that embarrassing moment safely forgotten, she hoped. So she was taken aback when Calum said, 'I understand you're a widow?'

Elaine's face hardened. 'Yes.' Her reply was short and crisp, not because she was still sensitive about the subject, but because she'd learned from experience where that kind of question usually led. Inwardly she cursed herself for having watched him, for letting him think that she might be attracted to him.

Tensely she waited for the inevitable proposition that always came after that question from a man, and was ready to tell him to get lost as forcefully as she knew how, even if it did cost her this job. But Calum said, 'And your business was entirely your own idea, and you've built it up yourself?'

'Yes.'

'You've done well. It must have been hard at times.'

Beginning to be puzzled, wondering whether she'd been wrong, but still cautious, Elaine answered, 'Yes, especially at the beginning.'

He looked at her expectantly, obviously presuming that she would enlarge further, but at that moment Francesca and Tiffany Dean came out on to the terrace. An interested light came into Calum's eyes as he looked at Tiffany and he immediately walked over to them.

He said, 'Francesca, do you have any further instructions for Mrs Beresford on the party at the *quinta*?'

Francesca nodded, although rather reluctantly, and when she went into the sitting-room with Elaine she stood in line with the terrace door so that she could look out to where Calum had now gone to sit next to Tiffany. She seemed abstracted, her attention more on the other two than on the papers she was supposed to be looking through. Her behaviour puzzled Elaine, until she thought of an obvious reason for it, then her eyes widened a little in surprise. Was Francesca jealous of the interest Calum was showing in Tiffany? Francesca had often spoken of her cousin, but it had never occurred to Elaine that she might feel more for him than a cousinly affection. But now Francesca made a move as if to go outside and confront the two of them, so Elaine said hastily, 'Do you know how many fado dancers and singers we'll have to cater for?'

With obvious reluctance, Francesca looked at a list and said, 'About twenty, I should think.' She added some more people, and then said, 'Oh, and the bullfighters and their assistants.'

Elaine stared at her incredulously, not having known they were having that kind of entertainment. 'Bullfighters?'

Francesca glanced at her, then said reassuringly, 'Oh, don't worry, we don't kill the bulls in Portugal. In fact, it's forbidden.'

'But the poor horses?'

'We won't use those either. The matadors will be on foot. It's rather like a ballet,' Francesca explained patiently. 'All very graceful and very harmless. Really. You must watch it.'

Mentally deciding that she would definitely give it a miss, Elaine made a note on her list. She went to ask another question, but Francesca was looking out on to the terrace again where Calum was laughing at something Tiffany had said. The angry look came into Francesca's eyes again, but just then her other cousin, Chris, came into the room and Francesca gave him an expressive but silent order to go outside and break it up.

He frowned, but did so, and it was interesting to see how annoyed Tiffany was to see him, although she covered it quickly and Calum didn't notice. So apparently there were two women who were interested in the heir to the Brodey empire, Elaine realised. Though she wouldn't have thought that either was right for Calum; the Brodeys were such a close family that marriage to Francesca would seem like incest, and Tiffany—well, she just didn't look right for the part.

'Elaine?'

She became aware that Francesca was waiting for her attention. 'Oh, sorry.'

They spent a further ten minutes or so discussing the details of the *quinta* party, then Francesca went outside to join the others. Elaine watched them for a few minutes, feeling herself to be the outsider, the looker-on. But interested for all that. But then, people were always interesting, especially if their basic feelings were aroused for some reason. Elaine found that she quite enjoyed watching others, especially as she always carefully fought down any feelings of her own.

She went back to Calum's office and typed out a detailed list of all that would be required for the big estate workers' party. They would need more cutlery and crockery, yet more glasses for the barrels of wine that would be drunk. It meant calling the local company that was supplying all these things, and no one there spoke any English. Picking up her lists again, Elaine went back to the sitting-room to get Francesca to put the call through for her.

Chris and Tiffany had gone, leaving the other two alone. They were sitting together on the wall surrounding the terrace and Calum had his arm round Francesca. As Elaine approached she saw Francesca give him a look of open entreaty. Calum drew her to him and kissed her. Admittedly, the kiss was on Francesca's forehead, not on her mouth, but the look she gave him in return was almost one of adoration.

Calum said something to her, then glanced up and saw Elaine. Immediately he let Francesca go and stood up. 'Here's Elaine looking for you again.' Was there a warning in his tone? Elaine wasn't sure.

Francesca made the call for her and Elaine went back to the kitchens, wondering if the cousins were having an affair. Was that why Calum hadn't married—because he

was in love with Francesca? But both of them were free,
so what was to stop them? Unless their grandfather had
put his foot down and forbidden it because of the close
family relationship. But would that make any difference
to two such self-assured people? If they loved their
grandfather it might, Elaine surmised. Or if they were
afraid of being cut out of his will.

She made sure that the preparations for dinner that
evening were in hand, then went into the dining-room
to put the name-cards into silver holders and set them
round the table, following the seating plan. This room,
like all the rooms in the *palácio*, was sumptuously fur-
nished with antique pieces that looked as if they'd been
there since the house was built—which they probably
had. Elaine spent a lot of time preparing the table, arranging a beautiful centre-piece of flowers which the
gardener had brought up for her. When she'd finished,
the table looked really beautiful, a fitting background
to this family celebration dinner.

Late that night, her work done and the family dinner
over, Elaine took a last look round the dining-room, then
went into the hall. The front door was opened by a key
and Calum came in. Elaine knew that the chauffeur had
been sent for earlier and that Calum had taken Tiffany
home. A host's politeness perhaps, or because he was
keen on the girl? He certainly couldn't have lingered; he
had been gone only long enough to drive into the city
and back. The thought strangely pleased Elaine.

Calum gave her a questioning look and nodded towards the folders she was carrying. 'You're not still
working, surely?'

'Just a few things I want to check over.'

'About the bicentennial? Can I help?' He put out an
arm as if to steer her into the library.

'No,' she said quickly. 'It's for some functions back in England.'

'You must learn to delegate,' Calum said with a smile. It was a very charming smile, and he hadn't taken his arm away. 'Come and have a nightcap?' he invited.

She hesitated, troubled, wondering if this was just well-mannered civility or whether he really wanted to. It flashed through her mind that it might be unwise to accept; not only was he her employer but he was also a very charismatic man. Having caught her watching him earlier, Calum might think that she was aware of him—as a man. He might make a pass. Might want to... Her thoughts fled in confused fright and she had to fight to stay calm. Fool! she chided herself the next instant; he's just got back from taking another girl home and this afternoon he was kissing Francesca. 'Thanks,' she said lightly. 'But it is very late.'

Calum gave a slow smile and Elaine had the distinct feeling that he could read her like an open book. A book that he'd read many times before and knew the text by heart? Was he that experienced with women, then?

'Of course. And you still have work to do, don't you?'

She thought she detected a touch of irony in his voice and said a hasty goodnight. He answered and she went on through the house, letting herself out of a side-door to cross the courtyard to her room. Sitting down at the desk, she opened the folders but found that she couldn't concentrate. Going to the window, she looked across at the house. Had Calum gone straight to bed, or was he having his nightcap? And who was he thinking of as he held the delicate crystal glass between long, capable fingers—herself or Tiffany Dean? A car went by on its way to the garage, and she recognised Francesca at the wheel. Everyone, it seemed, was busy tonight.

The following evening there was to be a party for the Brodey Corporation's local employees at their wine-lodge in Oporto. Elaine had been there once already to decide on the table layout, and had asked for a car to be available to take her there again early in the morning. At the specified time she came out of the house, dressed in her usual working outfit of trousers, with a sweater over a cotton shirt and her hair tied back in a thick plait, expecting to find one of the staff waiting to take her. Instead she found Calum standing by his car, and without his chauffeur, too.

He gave her his usual politely friendly smile. 'I'm going to the wine-lodge myself, so I thought I'd take you with me.'

'Thank you. I hope I haven't kept you waiting.'

'Not at all.'

He opened the passenger door for her and Elaine put on her dark glasses against the glare of the sun, which was still low on the horizon this early. She found that being alone with Calum disturbed her a little, so she quickly made some comment on the weather when he joined her and they chatted about nothing very much until they neared the town, when Calum had to concentrate on his driving. Elaine glanced at his hard profile— the high, lean cheekbones and strong, purposeful chin— trying to read the personality behind it. A very masculine kind of man, she thought. Standing no nonsense and probably quick to anger if he was crossed. She recognised the type. Neil had been in the Marines and many of his superior officers had been like that. Having spoken to Calum several times on the phone, she had already formed the opinion that he was authoritative, but actually meeting him when she had arrived in Portugal had been something of a shock: she hadn't expected anyone so young and so very good-looking.

She had quickly hidden her reaction, but supposed that many women must find him attractive; that he must be used to it. Involuntarily, she glanced into the back of the car, where Calum must have sat with Tiffany last night. What had they got up to? she wondered. Not much, of course, with the chauffeur there. But had he arranged to see the blonde girl again, to take her out to dinner as soon as he was free?

Elaine had hardly been out on a date since Neil had died, although there had been opportunities enough— and opportunities for far more than just a date. A grim look came to her face as she remembered some of the offers she'd received. And from Neil's so-called friends, too.

'Here we are.' Calum pulled into the wine-lodge and glanced at her. 'Is anything the matter?'

'What? Oh, no. I was—miles away.'

He frowned. 'It must be lonely for you here, I should have realised.'

'Oh, no—please,' she said in some alarm. 'I'm fine, Mr Brodey. Really.'

He gave her one of his charming smiles. 'Please call me Calum. Mr Brodey makes me feel on a par with my grandfather.'

She gave a polite murmur and got out of the car. Calum appointed one of the girls from the sale-room who spoke English to be her translator, and Elaine set to work to organise everything for that evening's function.

Calum was busy in his own office there for most of the morning, but at about twelve he came to look for her. He found her at the huge doors of the lodge, where the wine-barrels were loaded and unloaded, supervising the arrival of all the chairs which they had hired for the evening, the same chairs that had been used at the *palácio* the previous day and which would be taken by lorry to the *quinta* tomorrow.

'I'm going to have an early lunch, and I wondered if you'd care to join me.'

Elaine looked up from the clipboard she was holding, trying to hide her surprise, and gave him a smile which she hoped did not look harassed. When your client invites you to lunch, then you go, she reminded herself. 'I'll need to wash. Five minutes?'

He nodded. 'I'll be in my office.'

Finding Ned Talbot, the ex-head waiter she'd hired, Elaine explained and passed the job on to him, then quickly washed her hands, put on fresh lipstick, and joined Calum. He drove her down the steep hillside to the waterfront, to a café, one of several right on the riverside. They sat outside on a kind of pier, which jutted out over the river, at a table with a bright red cloth. The sun was hot even though it was only spring, and there was a continental atmosphere to their alfresco meal.

'These places specialise in fish caught fresh this morning,' Calum told her. 'You mustn't miss the opportunity to try some.'

'I'm afraid you'll have to translate the menu.'

He leaned closer, pointing with his finger as he went down the dishes. He was sitting opposite her and his knee brushed hers. She moved her legs aside but felt a *frisson* of sexuality that surprised and disturbed her. Even if he had been interested, even if he hadn't already got his hands full with Francesca and Tiffany, this was no man for her. She wondered why he'd invited her to lunch—out of politeness, perhaps? But then she remembered his remark earlier about her being lonely. He'd asked her out of a sense of duty, then, taking pity on the poor widow they'd hired. Immediately she felt a fierce stab of anger. She neither wanted nor needed his compassion. She had her own business and her own life; no way was she to be pitied.

'I'll have that one,' she said shortly, stabbing at the menu and cutting him off abruptly.

Calum glanced up, about to say something, but stopped short when he saw the flame of anger in her eyes. 'Er—yes, of course. And I think we'll have a *vinho verde* to go with it.' Calling the waiter over, he gave the order, then glanced at her again.

But Elaine had regained her self-control now. There was just casual interest in her eyes as she pointed to the *barcos rabelos* with their cargoes of empty wine-barrels which she could see moored further along the river. 'Do they ever sail, or are they just moored here all the time, for the tourists?'

'Oh, yes, they still sail. Every year we have a race from the river-mouth back here to the main quay. All the port companies compete and there are great festivities in the town—lots of drinking and fireworks in the evening.'

He was watching her as he spoke, curiosity in his gaze, but she had herself well in hand and didn't let him see into her soul again.

'And do you ever win?'

He smiled. 'It has been known. My cousins always come over for the race and we crew it with some men from the company.'

'You race it yourselves?' Elaine said in surprise, not having expected him to be the type and having to do some mental revision.

'Why, yes. Grandfather always took us along as soon as we were old enough. But unfortunately he's too old to go now.'

There was true regret in his voice, and she realised he was genuinely fond of the old patriarch. 'That's a shame,' she murmured.

He nodded, but gave a sudden grin that was so different from his usual polite smile that it startled her. 'Yes, but he always comes to cheer us along, and I think he expends more energy doing that than he would if he was with us crewing the boat.'

The waiter brought the wine and Calum turned away, leaving Elaine free to marvel at the change in him, to wonder whether there were depths to his character that he didn't often show. But then she shrugged off the thought. What did it matter what Calum Brodey was like? He was merely a customer she had to be polite to, to keep happy until this week was over and he had paid her astronomical bill. His other side was none of her business, even though he seemed more interesting every time she met him.

She found that she'd ordered a dish of squid cooked with minced ham and onion in a tomato sauce: tasty but filling. During the meal Calum told her something of the history of the wine-lodge, and so of his own family. He made the story fascinating, describing the misfortunes that had hit his ancestors when they'd first come here, and told it so graphically that he made it seem like yesterday.

'You ought to write a book about your family,' she remarked.

He gave her an interested glance. 'Do you think so? We have all the family records at home, of course, but no one has ever attempted to collate them. I suppose we're all so used to the stories that we take them for granted.'

'I think it would make an absorbing book.'

He acknowledged the tacit compliment to his ability as a raconteur with a nod. 'Perhaps you're right. Maybe I'll give it some thought.' But then Calum gave a rueful smile. 'If I ever have time.'

'Doesn't your grandfather have time?'

She had his whole attention now. 'My grandfather?'

'Surely he knows more about your family history than anyone? If he doesn't feel up to going through the archives and writing it up, then don't you think he could write down his own story? That would be interesting for all your family and a must for anyone in the future who wanted to write a history of the House of Brodey.'

'What an excellent idea. I'm sure that Grandfather will be feeling very flat once this week is over; I'll put it to him then. It will give him a new interest.' He gave her a warm smile. 'Thank you, Elaine. I'm grateful.'

She shrugged. 'It was the way you told me about your family that gave me the idea.'

She had eaten only half her meal and drunk sparingly of the wine; she didn't like heavy lunches when she was working, and never drank very much anyway. But she had enjoyed this lunch, which was strange because she hadn't expected to. Maybe it was sitting outside in the sun. Or maybe it was because of her companion.

Calum glanced at his watch. 'I'd better get you back to the wine-lodge. I have to be back at the house this afternoon.'

'Will you be working in your office there?' Elaine asked. 'I'm expecting a fax and I wondered if you could telephone it through to me,' she explained.

'I'll arrange for it to be done,' he told her. 'We're expecting Tiffany to call so I might be busy myself.'

'Oh, of course.'

So he *had* made a date with Tiffany. It surprised her, though, that it was for the afternoon and at the house. Somehow Elaine had expected Calum at least to take his dates out to dinner. But then she remembered that he was a well-known and important figure in Oporto; maybe he didn't want to be seen in public with Tiffany yet, didn't want to give the gossips something to talk about.

Calum dropped her at the wine-lodge and lifted a hand in a casual wave as he drove on. Elaine watched him go, this handsome man in his sleek car, heading eagerly for a date with his blonde. Had he found the love of his life? she wondered. The fair English girl that his family tradition demanded? Well, whether he had or not, it was nothing to do with her.

Shrugging, Elaine went into the wine-lodge to get back to work, but again she found it difficult to concentrate and had to give herself a mental ticking-off before she could put Calum out of her mind.

CHAPTER TWO

BY ABOUT four Elaine had done as much work at the wine-lodge as she could before the actual event, so she and Ned Talbot took a taxi back to the *palácio*, intending to have a rest before the evening. Her chef, Malcolm Webster, was overseeing the preparation of the food in the kitchens of a nearby hotel and had telephoned in to say that all was going well.

Calum hadn't telephoned her fax message through so Elaine went along to his office to see if it had arrived. It had, so it would appear that he was too engrossed in his date with Tiffany to have remembered her request. The fax was from London, detailing some changes that were being made for a business function for which she had already quoted. The organisers, of course, wanted her revised estimate urgently, so she spent the next hour sitting at the desk working it out. She was just typing it all out to fax through when Ned came in with tea on a tray.

'I thought you'd like a decent cup of tea,' he told her. 'The people here don't know how to make it properly even though they work for an English family.'

'Have you had a rest, Ned?'

'I napped for a while.' He leaned towards her. 'There's great excitement here. They're all talking about it in the staffroom.'

Elaine smiled; trust Ned to hear all the gossip, even if it was in a foreign language. He was in his forties, glossily clean, and still slim and pleasantly good-looking. He was single, and when she'd first hired him she'd been afraid that he might run after the waitresses, but soon found that he and Malcolm, the chef, were an item and had been for years. Now she had taken both men on to her permanent staff and all three of them worked in perfect harmony.

'Why, what's happened?' she asked, knowing he would tell her anyway.

'You know that big American—the one who got his face slapped at the party yesterday? It seems the Princess invited him here this afternoon at the same time as the girl who hit him. In the kitchen they're saying that the girl and the American probably cooked up the whole thing between them. They said that there have been several girls over the years who've tried to attract Calum one way or another.'

'Well, he seems to have fallen for this one,' Elaine remarked.

Ned shook his head. 'No, Calum sent for his car and the girl's been taken home.'

'He didn't go with her?'

'No, the chauffeur took her.'

So Francesca had spiked that budding romance, Elaine thought as she stirred her tea. She wondered how Calum would feel about it, and whether he would turn against Francesca for having spoiled it for him. But it was a risk the Princess had obviously been prepared to take. A thought occurred to her. 'Didn't the American leave with the girl?'

'No. They said he left later in his own car.' Realising what that implied, Ned said, 'So maybe he and the girl didn't plot it between them. Maybe she used him.'

It would seem that the latter theory was right, because when the family arrived at the wine-lodge that evening the American, Sam Gallagher, was with them. He was evidently a last-minute addition to the guest-list because

Elaine hadn't been told about him. Calum sought her out as soon as he arrived and, with a wry smile, asked her to set another place. He added, interestingly, 'At least we know about this extra person; he isn't a gate-crasher like the last time.'

'The last time?' Elaine questioned.

'Yes. It seems that Tiffany Dean crashed the garden party,' Calum said tersely. His mouth twisted, and for a moment there was a bleak look in his eyes, but then he recovered and said, 'I blamed you for not setting enough places, didn't I? I'm sorry.'

She shrugged, interested to see how it had affected him. 'It's nothing.'

Calum gave a short, wry laugh. 'As you say—it's nothing.'

He went back to join his family in the big room where the tourists came to taste the wines, cleared now of the tables and stools made from old barrels, except for one central table piled high with flowers which Elaine had arranged earlier. Waiting to greet the family were all their employees at the wine-lodge, as well as a great many other local people with whom they had business dealings. The Brodeys seemed to be held in great respect, Elaine noticed as she watched from a doorway, but there was no humility among the employees; owners and workers alike greeted each other with smiles and laughter, like old friends.

As soon as everyone had shaken hands, Elaine gave a signal and the waiters went round with large trays of white port. There were a couple of speeches in Portuguese, then everyone moved out into the huge wine cellars where a special cask was to be broached. These cellars had been a revelation to Elaine: so vast, so high and old, the smell of hundreds of years of maturing wine so strong that you could feel drunk on that alone.

More wine was poured and handed round, empty glasses had to be refilled. Elaine, standing unobtrusively in the background in her neat black velvet evening skirt and short jacket, kept an alert eye on it all, making sure that everything went smoothly. She had worked hard on the setting for this meal, taking the unusual surroundings as a challenge, and transforming the gloomy cellars into a warm and inviting bistro with brightly coloured tablecloths, lamps and candles. But there was nothing cheap about it: the glass was crystal, the plates the finest bone china. And beside each place-setting there was a gift of a wine glass engraved with the date and event, parcels that she had helped wrap herself.

A band of local musicians arrived and soon everyone was dancing, including Francesca, who literally let her hair down as she whirled around the floor, joining in the local folk dances with a young Portuguese. The male Brodeys didn't dance so much, only doing so if it was a western number, when they dutifully asked the wives of some of their guests and employees.

But Calum had no duty towards Elaine when he asked her to dance. She had come into the cellar to replace some candles which were spluttering and was about to leave when he came over to her. 'Elaine? Would you care to dance?'

She looked at him in surprise, only now registering that the band was playing a slow number that she recognised from the charts of ten years ago. Guessing that he had again asked her out of pity, she said at once, 'Thank you, but I'm very busy.'

She went to walk past him, but he put a hand on her arm. Giving her one of his charming smiles, he said, 'Surely you can take a few minutes off?'

Her heart jumped a little as she thought of being held in his arms, but stubborn pride made her say curtly, 'Sorry. No.'

The smile didn't falter. 'But I insist.' His grip tightened on her arm and he took a step towards the cleared space where people were dancing, drawing her after him.

Good God, couldn't the man take no for an answer? Did he think he was doing her a favour, playing the rich man being kind to the lonely little hireling? Her face stiffening, striving to contain her anger but failing, Elaine stood her ground. Calum looked back and became still as he saw the fire in her glance. Tersely, she said, 'Thank you, Mr Brodey, but I don't dance.' And, tugging her arm from his hold, she strode quickly away.

But at the door to the cellar she couldn't resist glancing back. She expected Calum to have moved away already, to do his duty or be kind to some other female, but he was still standing where she had left him, looking after her with a coldly surprised expression on his handsome face.

She didn't go into the big cellar again until the members of the family had left. The band played on for a while but Elaine left them to it, arranging for the senior employee at the wine-lodge to shut up the premises when the last guest had gone. It had been a long day and she was tired. Ned and Malcolm had already left, but one of the staff from the *palácio* drove her back there. It would have been nice to go straight to her room and bed, but Elaine went first to Calum's office to see if there were any messages for her; taking on a week's celebrations like this was lucrative but it was difficult to run her own office in London from such a distance.

Several messages had come through to the house on the fax machine, and some by telephone. Only two of them were for her, one acknowledging receipt of the faxed estimate she had sent earlier, the other from her mother-in-law inviting her to a family birthday party, and adding, 'And perhaps you might like to arrange it.'

She wouldn't go, of course; her mother-in-law should have realised that by now. But perhaps the older woman thought it her duty to ask her and had added that last sentence to nag Elaine's conscience, to make her think of the duty she was supposed to owe Neil's family. But Elaine was quite sure that she owed them nothing whatsoever—not duty, and certainly not affection or love. Her face grim, she crumpled the paper into a tight ball. As she did so, the door opened and Calum came in.

He paused when he saw her. 'I saw the light was on and wondered who was here,' he explained. He gave her a guarded look, evidently remembering the way she'd snubbed him earlier.

'I came to see if there were any messages for me.'

Calum gave a rueful sigh, impatient with himself. 'I'm sorry, I said I'd look earlier today, didn't I? I'm afraid— something happened and it went out of my mind.' He frowned. 'But surely you were in here this afternoon?'

'Yes, I received that message. I wanted to see if there was any problem with my answer to it.' She flicked the ball of paper neatly into a waste-paper basket. 'Goodnight.' She went to leave.

'One moment.' He lifted a hand to stop her.

Elaine hesitated, then turned to face him. 'Yes? You have some instructions for me?' she asked in her most businesslike manner.

'No. I merely wished to say...' His eyes, grey and quizzical, met hers. 'Well, that I hope I didn't offend you when I asked you to dance this evening.'

'Offend me? No, of course not,' she lied.

He was watching her and she was uncomfortably aware that he didn't believe her, and he proved it by saying, 'I don't usually get that reaction when I ask someone to dance.'

'I was busy,' she prevaricated.

'You were furious,' he countered. 'Now, why, I wonder?'

'Not at all,' she said dismissively, and turned to the door.

But Calum was standing in the way and didn't move. 'Have you never danced?'

She thought of refusing to answer, but then said stiffly, 'Yes, of course.'

'Then I must have seriously offended you—and I'm extremely sorry. I didn't mean to—awaken old memories.'

Elaine stared at him speechlessly, realising he was referring to supposed memories of her dead husband that dancing might have evoked. Realised, too, that he was watching her keenly to see if he was right. She suddenly found his presence, his overbearing masculinity, too much, and said shortly, 'If you'll excuse me, Mr Brodey, I think I'll go to my room. I'm very tired.'

A frown flickered in his brows, but he murmured, 'Of course,' and moved out of the doorway. But as she went to pass him he put a hand on her arm and said, 'I thought we'd agreed that you'd call me Calum.'

She found, unnervingly, that his touch sent a tremor of awareness sighing through her veins. But somehow she managed to control it and her voice was light, casual, as she said, 'So we did. Goodnight, then, Calum.'

'Goodnight, Elaine. I hope you sleep well.'

But when Elaine got into bed she lay awake for some time. Trying to ignore her stupid reaction to his touch, she went over that conversation in his study, wondering why Calum had bothered with her at all. Was it that he was piqued because she'd refused to dance with him?

Did he expect all women to fall for his charm and good looks? Which they probably did, she thought cynically. Well, that made him a male chauvinist of the first order, as far as Elaine was concerned. She had seen too much of that type, lived with one for too long, and now had no time for it. In her case, it was once bitten forever shy.

Inevitably, her thoughts drifted back to the time when she had met Neil, nearly ten years ago. She had been so young then, only eighteen, innocent, impressionable. But Neil had been over thirty, a success in his chosen career, fully adult in every sense of the word. He had literally swept her off her feet, knocking into her one day at the tennis club, when he had run from his court into the next to hit a lob, and cannoned into her. She had fallen, and Neil, she remembered, had hit the lob back and scored the point before he'd turned to help her up. An action that was typical of him, although she hadn't realised it for quite some time.

He had been staying with friends while on leave, but spent the rest of the time pursuing her—there was no other word for it—determined to capture Elaine's heart as quickly as possible. He had done so quite easily; she had been overwhelmed by him, had never before met anyone with his masterful assertiveness, his clean-cut good looks, his easy charm. They had been married only a few months after they met, and it had been quite a lot later before she'd found out that his masterfulness hid an iron determination always to have his own way. His good looks attracted other women of whom he took full advantage, and his charm was used to make the lies he told acceptable, even believable.

Since then she had become extremely wary of any man who had any one of those qualities—and Calum Brodey had all three, in abundance. Which gave her every reason to steer well clear of him, even if all he felt towards her was a sort of conscience-pricked pity.

Elaine turned restlessly on her pillow, cross with herself for having even thought of Calum. It was, she realised, going to be one of those nights. Switching on the bedside lamp, she sat up and leaned against a pillow, picked up a novel which she kept for nights like these. But tonight reading didn't work, didn't leave her with buzzing eyes and a mind so tired that nothing would keep her awake. Her mind drifted from the book to that almost peremptory invitation from her mother-in-law. Again resentment filled her. Neil's mother had always known he was a womaniser. She might have expected, if not hoped, that marriage to an innocent teenager would change him, but hadn't cared in the least when it hadn't. Neil might have been faithful for a year or so, but Elaine strongly doubted if it had been more than that.

She hadn't known at the time, of course; Neil had been away a lot, taking courses and things, and he had been so ardent when he came home that she had been completely fooled. It had only been towards the end, when he'd had a post near home but was forever making excuses to be away, that she had begun to suspect. She had been pregnant at the time.

Lonely one weekend, because Neil was away—at a conference, he'd said—she'd thought she would please him by taking a couple of his suits to the cleaners. Going through his pockets, she'd found a hotel bill made out to Mr and Mrs Beresford. A hotel in a well-known chain, situated in a suburban town not too far away; a hotel at which she had never stayed, the bill dated at a time when Neil was supposed to have been on a course nowhere near that town. The kind of outdoor training course for new recruits where he was never near a phone, definitely not available, so she had never tried to contact him.

Trying to convince herself that she was wrong, Elaine rang the hotel and asked if Mr and Mrs Beresford were staying there again. She was told they were. For hours she walked round the house, wondering, trying to convince herself that there was some mistake; it wasn't true. In the end she got in the car and drove over to the hotel, knowing that she had to see for herself. Only when she reached it did it occur to Elaine that finding out might not be so easy. The receptionist might not give her Neil's room number; he might have gone out. Even with this terrible suspicion in her mind, she couldn't bring herself to think of *their* room, that *they* might have gone out.

In the end it was terribly easy. It was late evening and the hotel entrance was deserted, the guests either out or eating in the restaurant. Looking through the glass doors of the latter, Elaine saw Neil sitting with a blonde girl. Even as she watched they rose to leave. Quickly, her mind panicking, Elaine hid in a darkened telephone booth. They passed quite close to her as they came out into the lobby and she saw that the blonde was very curvacious, her breasts almost falling out of her tight red dress. Neil had his arm round her and kissed her neck lasciviously as they waited for a lift. The girl giggled—and reached out to stroke him! Neil's head came up and he looked round, making Elaine shrink back in her hiding place. Seeing no one, he put his hand over the girl's and pressed it against himself.

The lift came and they got into it, Neil pulling the girl close, his hands low on her hips, even before the doors had closed.

For several minutes Elaine couldn't move, then she rushed into the ladies' room and was horribly ill. Immediately afterwards she ran blindly back to the car and drove away as fast as she could, tears streaming down her face. So much for her perfect marriage; so much for trust and love; so much for the father of this child she was carrying, the baby she had longed for for so long—years. Sobbing wildly, wiping the tears from her eyes so that she could see, Elaine just kept going, not caring where she was heading, only knowing that she couldn't go home, that it wasn't her home any more, the place on which she had lavished such loving care. All for Neil! All for Neil! Now it was just the place he came back to when he wasn't with that girl!

She didn't feel anger, not then; she felt only shame and a terrible certainty that it must be her fault, that he would never have gone to bed with someone else unless she had failed him sexually. That side of their marriage had not been a success right from the start. Neil had been a selfish lover, always taking his own pleasure, any excitement she might feel being incidental. He had wanted her to do things that she found unnatural and which she'd resisted, but instead of persuading her Neil had forced her to do them. She'd become afraid of sex, unable to relax, and Neil had got angry and hurt her, accused her of being frigid. During the first few years of their marriage she had blamed herself entirely; she hadn't known that not every man treated sex almost as an assault course and left their wives bruised and frustrated. But she still loved him because she thought that she had made him behave like it.

That terrible night, Elaine found herself driving down an unlit country road. A car rounded a bend towards her, going fast, its headlights dazzling her. It hooted at her angrily. Her eyes blurred by tears, she swerved to avoid it, and ended up in a ditch. The other driver didn't stop. She wasn't hurt but it took an effort to climb out of the car and back on to the road. She waited for some time, expecting another car to come by, but the road stayed dark, deserted. Soon it began to rain. She began to get cold and had to climb into the car again and get her jacket and handbag. Reaching to where it had fallen, she felt a pain in her stomach.

Having no idea where she was, Elaine grimly began to walk to the nearest house so that she could phone a garage. But there was no house for miles and she ended up in a phone box, dialling for an ambulance, curled up in pain and knowing that she was losing her baby.

She didn't tell Neil the truth about what had happened; never told him. And he never found out. By the time he had been 'traced' at his so-called conference, she was in hospital, the car retrieved by the AA and brought home with only a dented wing to show for what had happened. She told him she'd skidded off the road to avoid a cat when she was going shopping, the morning after she'd seen him with the girl. He didn't bother to check her story, blamed her for what happened, yelling that she was a bloody rotten driver, that she ought to have had more sense and driven over the cat rather than avoid it. His parents blamed her too, and left her in no doubt of their feelings.

Neil was genuinely upset over the loss of the baby, Elaine was sure of that; he accused her of killing it often enough. Not that he needed to: as it was she felt consumed by guilt. She tried to make it up to him by taking better care of him: his clothes were always beautifully laundered, his meals cooked to perfection, and when he wanted sex she forced herself to be especially warm, especially loving; she even tried to please him by doing some of the things she found so abhorrent. But it seemed that wasn't what he wanted from her any more. He told her to stop acting like a cheap tramp; she was his wife, for God's sake!

The anger came back then, and the next time he took her she just lay there, not resisting but not taking part, her mind completely detached. That seemed to anger Neil even more, but he soon got tired of it, soon left her alone. He began to go away a lot more, sometimes staying away for weeks at a time. He had taken up flying, but never took her with him. Then one day he tried to do an acrobatic manoeuvre: it didn't work, and he crashed the plane and was killed.

Shocked and stunned by his death, Elaine took a couple of months to get round to going through his desk. There were the usual papers, but in a locked drawer she found his diaries. It was all there, fully detailed and sometimes illustrated with erotic photographs—accounts of his affairs with women, some long-lasting, some one-night stands. Among the names, the faces in the photographs above the naked bodies, were some she recognised—girls she had thought to be her friends, wives of his fellow officers, even the barmaid from the local pub.

It had gone on for years. She looked back at the diaries for the years before he had met her and it had been going on then too. It was obvious from the comments when he had got some girl into trouble and his mother had bailed him out that she knew, had always known, even after he and Elaine were married. There was one very telling comment:

> Ma was bragging about how I took one of the girls to bed at her anniversary party, right from under Elaine's nose, while she was clearing the food away. It wasn't a bad lay, although the girl was a bit tipsy. Can't remember her name.

Reading through the diaries up until her wedding, Elaine realised she seemed to be the only one of his women that he hadn't made love to at the first available opportunity. Maybe it had amused him to keep her a virgin until their wedding night. The diaries for the two years after her marriage she couldn't bear to look at. Still couldn't, she mused now. But she had kept them all, and whenever she felt down she read them, fuelling her strength and determination from the anger they created in her.

All grief gone, her heart a hard ball in her chest, Elaine had immediately sold the house, bought a small flat in London, and started her business on the remaining capital. Her mother-in-law had strongly objected, evidently expecting her to grieve like a dutiful widow for the rest of her life. But anger had given her life and still sustained her, so that tonight she had been able to treat Neil's mother's invitation with the contempt that she felt for the woman herself.

The next morning Elaine woke feeling heavy-eyed, but had to pull herself together and pack some clothes to take with her to the *quinta* where she would be staying for a couple of nights. She did some paperwork while she ate a belated breakfast, making out fresh check-lists and going through others, ticking off what had been done and underlining things that were becoming urgent. Afterwards she had a conference with Ned and Malcolm, making sure that they knew what they had to do.

This done, Elaine took her case out to the main hall and went to look for Francesca. She found her in the sitting-room talking to Michel, and would have excused herself but Francesca beckoned her in.

'Oh, there you are, Elaine. I'm all ready to leave.'

'Where are you going?' Michel wanted to know.

'To the *quinta*. We're going on ahead to prepare for tomorrow's party.'

Michel immediately offered to drive them there, but Francesca refused and they went out to her open-topped sports car. Michel hovered around, looking sulky, but Francesca merely said, 'Goodbye, Michel. Maybe I'll see you around some time.'

She drove down towards Oporto, crossing the road bridge and turning on to the road that wound along beside the river. When they were out of the town, Francesca gave a sigh. 'Have you ever done something that you regretted immediately afterwards?'

Elaine laughed. 'Loads of times. Why, what have you done?'

'Invited Michel to spend the week here. I can't think why I did it. Because I thought I'd be lonely, I suppose. And because he made it clear that he so much wanted to come that he made me feel guilty.' She glanced at Elaine, saw the wind playing with tendrils of red hair that had come loose from the rather severe style she habitually wore. 'You're so sure of yourself; I'm sure you don't really make mistakes like that.'

'I used to,' Elaine admitted, thinking back. 'But I don't now. I never let anyone use moral blackmail on me, and I don't do anything that I don't want to.'

'Good heavens!' Francesca's eyebrows rose at the hardness in her tone. 'What made you like that?'

'I went to an assertiveness training course for women. It did me a great deal of good.'

'So it sounds. Maybe that's what I need.'

'Well, you were quite terse with Michel; he surely won't hang around after that?'

'I hope not. But there are some men you just can't get rid of, aren't there?' Elaine was silent, wondering if Francesca wanted to get rid of Michel so that she would be free to continue her affair with Calum. But the Princess mistook her silence and after a moment said,

'Sorry, Elaine. I'm not being very tactful, am I, boring on about boyfriends?'

'It doesn't bother me.'

Francesca gave her an interested glance. 'How long is it since your husband was killed?'

'Nearly three years.'

'You must miss him terribly.' Again Elaine didn't answer, so Francesca took her silence for assent. A strangely wistful look came into her eyes, and she said, 'I suppose when you've had a loving, happy marriage it must be terribly hard to adjust. You must feel that there could never be anyone who could possibly take your husband's place?'

'Oh, quite,' Elaine agreed with hidden irony. Francesca was right: no one could take Neil's place, because she was going to make darn sure that no man ever did. She neither trusted nor needed them and was perfectly happy and fulfilled on her own. But then she remembered the *frisson* of sexual awareness that Calum had aroused in her and she felt suddenly unsure of herself. But it was only for the briefest moment, and then she sternly told herself that an occasional lapse was only natural; she was still young after all, and her femininity hadn't died just because Neil had turned out to be a lying cheat. OK, so she hadn't felt anything like that in years, but she supposed that it would be bound to happen, now and again, until she'd managed to stifle any sexuality she had left. Not wanting to talk about men, she pointed across the river. 'What beautiful scenery.'

It wasn't just an idle remark—the view across the Douro was outstanding, the rolling hills a rich patchwork of almond and cherry blossom, with here and there the white walls and red pantiled roof of a house, many of them in the baroque style, like the *palácio*. The land seemed to be very fertile, with lots of trees and bushes in every shade of green.

'There aren't so many trees further upriver,' Francesca told her. 'The hills are covered in grape-vines. Hundreds of thousands of them.'

They passed two dams on the river, higher than Elaine had ever seen, and then they began to see the vines, stretching, as Francesca had said, in row upon row over the hillsides, for as far as the eye could see. 'Do all these belong to the Brodey House?' she asked in awe.

'No.' Francesca laughed. 'These belong to other wine companies. Our *quinta* is further along, near Pinhao.'

She pointed the boundary out when they reached it, but to Elaine they still seemed to go on for miles before they left the main road and drove up a long avenue on the side of a hill, following its contours, circling between the vines, and eventually coming to a stone gateway. There was nothing pretentious about it, just two pillars of weathered pink stone, curved at the top, with open-work iron gates hung between them under an arch bearing the name 'Quinta dos Colinas'.

'What does it mean?' Elaine asked.

'Roughly, farm of the hills.'

A man came running to open the gates, shouting something to Francesca, a big smile on his face. She called back and, looking at her, Elaine thought how relaxed she suddenly seemed.

The house at the *quinta* was delightful, just two-storeyed, with balconies that stretched the whole width of the house on the side overlooking the distant river, the side facing south. Like most of the houses in the area it was painted white, and was surrounded by a garden thick with trees and flowering shrubs. Elaine would have liked to look round the gardens but there was no time; after she'd been shown to her room and unpacked the few things she'd brought with her, she was immediately plunged into preparations for the party.

Rather to Elaine's surprise, Francesca was a willing and efficient helper, making phone calls, translating her orders, and they were both kept busy all that day and most of the next. Francesca was annoyed to see that Michel had decided to come, despite her snub. He arrived early the next morning with all the male Brodeys. Despite her will-power, Elaine again had to ignore an increased beat of her heart when she saw Calum. It seemed he was no longer angry with Francesca, because he greeted his cousin with a hug, and she immediately coerced him into helping to carry tables and benches. But she did that to her other cousins too, so that anyone who hadn't seen them together as Elaine had wouldn't have thought she had any preference for Calum.

It was a warm day and got progressively hotter. Lorry-loads of tables and benches and chairs had to be unloaded and set in place. There were barrels of wine and hundreds of glasses to be laid out, tiers of seats to be set round the makeshift bullring, and a stage for the fado dancers to be built. There were enough willing helpers but as Elaine went backwards and forwards from the house she noticed that the Brodeys were all working with the rest of the men. Calum was wearing faded jeans and a sweatshirt, the sleeves pushed up to reveal tanned skin and useful muscles.

There seemed to be good-humoured banter among the men as they worked, lots of laughter. A young vineyard worker next to Calum, probably urged on by his elders, tried to carry a case of wine on his shoulder and promptly dropped it. Elaine expected Calum to round on the boy and be angry, but he merely laughed and made some remark that made the other men roar and the boy give a rueful grin. It occurred to Elaine that if Neil had seen one of his young recruits do something like that he would have bawled him out in front of everyone and probably put him to doing degrading jobs for a week as a punishment.

After a brief stop for lunch, when everyone sat beneath the nearest tree, the work went on until, by the early afternoon, all was near enough ready. Most of the men went home to change into their best clothes, but a few stayed to build and light the fires beneath the spits on which the meat was to be roasted. Elaine took the opportunity to go to her room to wash and tidy herself, but heard another large vehicle arriving and went quickly out in case she was needed. As she came out of her room she bumped straight into Calum.

For a moment she didn't know it was him. He was halfway through pulling off his shirt, now wet with perspiration, and it was covering his head.

'Oh!' Elaine put out her hands to protect herself and found them pressed against a broad naked chest.

Calum pulled the shirt over his head and a strong smell of wood-smoke from its folds filled her nostrils—that and the muskiness of male sweat from hard exertion. His skin was hot under her hands, the down of hairs on his chest, a darker shade than on his head, clinging damply as they circled and embraced his tiny, masculine nipples. His shoulders were broad, powerful and well-proportioned. His arms were strong and muscular. Seeing him in his businesslike dark suits, one would never have guessed that his body could be so beautiful.

'Elaine! I'm so sorry. Did I hurt you?' There was a smudge of soot from the fire on his cheek where he had rubbed sweat from his eyes with the back of his hand. Perspiration had made his usually thick straight hair damp and curly, making him look younger, more carefree.

A great surge of desire suddenly filled her, taking Elaine by surprise, making her eyes widen, her lips part in aroused awareness. For a moment her whole body felt primeval in its intense need, as if every basic instinct woman had ever known had come alive inside her.

She blinked and stepped back, lowering her head, afraid that he had seen. 'No. It was—it was my fault. Excuse me.' She hurriedly stepped past him and went on her way.

The vehicle was a high-sided lorry bringing the bull for the *tourada*. It was greeted with shouts of enthusiasm from the locals, who crowded round the rather nondescript-looking men who had come with it in the lorry and in an old car that followed behind. The bull— big, black and powerful—looked angry enough, but then what animal wouldn't after having been driven on uneven roads in the sun? It was led off and Elaine followed at a safe distance to make sure the poor creature had some shade, and food and water. But the men with it looked after the bull before going to have a drink themselves, leaving it resting under a thatched outbuilding.

Instead of going back to the house, Elaine walked out among the grape-vines, following a track that led up the hillside. There was no shade—the vines were too low, only waist-high, and any trees that might have grown there had long since been felled to make way for the all-important vines. She could see the bunches of grapes forming on them, still small and green, needing a few months more of rain and sun to ripen them into the juicy black fruit from which the port would be made. When she'd gone for a couple of hundred yards, she turned to look back at the house.

Usually it must have been a very peaceful scene—the white house, long and low, nestling in its green garden, the outhouses of the small winery—or *adega* as Francesca called it—standing a short distance away. Here there was no swimming-pool, no ornamental lake or landscaped lawns or flowerbeds. It all seemed very natural in its setting, to have evolved over the years and settled peacefully in its fold in the hills, to lie somnolent beneath the sun and the cloudless blue of the sky. It was as different from the *palácio* in Oporto as Calum was different here from the businessman who ran his family's empire with such acumen. It was basic, earthy, carefree, just as he seemed to be today.

Closing her eyes to feel the sun on her face, Elaine's mind, her senses, all went back to that moment in the corridor. His skin had felt so silky; she had wanted to keep her hands on him, to stroke him. It had taken an effort to step away, to hide the sensual awareness that had filled her at that moment. But it was still there, that feeling, as she recalled it so vividly. Even the scent of wood-smoke on his shirt was there. She could see again the sweat that clung to his skin, knew that if she'd licked it from her fingers it would have tasted of the salt from his body.

A tremor ran through her and Elaine moved restlessly. She'd forgotten how beautiful the naked body of a man could be, how it had thrilled her once all those years ago, when she'd been a virgin, teenage bride. How strange that it should happen to her again now, nearly ten years later. But then, it had been so long since she'd had a man. Or rather since a man had had her—because she had never got any excitement out of sex. All those years she'd been married she had known nothing but pain and frustration, although sometimes she'd pretended excitement because she'd known that that was what Neil wanted, what fed his ego. But she couldn't have been very good at it because Neil had seen through her pretence every time, and then had punished her until she cried, all the while calling her a frigid bitch, a cold, sexless cow.

Pushing the sound of his yelling voice from her mind, Elaine tried to recapture that first thrill on seeing a man naked for the first time. But with it had gone all Neil's other characteristics which she had grown to hate, faults which she was pretty sure Calum also had. So whatever she felt when he was near, whatever desires rose in her wayward body, she must make every effort to fight them down. Men weren't to be trusted. And they were no longer necessary in a woman's life.

But, as Elaine walked back towards the house, she couldn't help feeling again that moment when she had been just a woman succumbing to her natural reactions, her overwhelming need for a man.

CHAPTER THREE

IT WAS a wild party! The guests began to arrive in a steady stream, driving up to the *quinta* in all kinds of vehicles, from families in carts pulled by bedecked horses, to leather-clad young men on powerful motorcycles, usually with a girl clinging on behind.

There seemed to be no check on whether the people had been officially invited or had invited themselves; all were made welcome and went to the bullring to get a good seat. Elaine heard the great roar when it started from inside the house. She was in the kitchen, watching not only her paid assistants but also all the local women who had come to offer their services and were happily helping with the food and talking at the tops of their voices. She stood by rather helplessly, not wanting to turn anyone away because they obviously wanted and expected to give a hand, but there were far too many people in the kitchen, large though it was. Malcolm, her chef, was there too, and having a lovely time bossing all the women about, not that they understood a word he was saying.

Francesca, wearing a silk sun-top and a gorgeous full skirt in a kaleidoscope of colours, came into the kitchen looking for her. 'Come on, come and see,' she said, taking Elaine's arm and drawing her towards the door.

'The bullfight? No, Francesca, it's really not my scene.'

'How do you know until you've seen it?' Francesca said reasonably. 'It really isn't gory. I wouldn't watch it if it was. Just have a look,' she coaxed.

53

Reluctantly, Elaine went with her. The two girls made a striking contrast as they walked along. Francesca was the taller of the two, the difference in height accentuated because she was wearing high, platform sandals, whereas Elaine had on sensible flat working shoes. Francesca's golden hair was loose around her shoulders, Elaine restrained hers in a coil at her neck. The Princess was all colour and richness, wearing jewels even to this kind of party, but Elaine wore a short-sleeved linen dress in a pale green colour. It was smart enough but subdued, designed to keep her in the background where she belonged and wanted to stay.

Only when one looked at their faces were the two women equal. Both had good bone-structure, with straight noses and high cheekbones, but Francesca's skin was tanned, her eyes grey and enhanced by make-up. Elaine had a much softer appeal; her copper-red hair meant a delicate skin which didn't take kindly to too much sun. Her eyes were green like the sea, her long lashes like the soft palm-fronds that graced the shore. Her mouth, with its full lower lip, seemed always to be trembling on the edge of a smile, a smile that you were somehow sure would light up and transform her face.

Old Mr Brodey and some older people were sitting under the shade of an awning, but the rest of the spectators were sitting out in the afternoon sun on the benches that formed the bullring. The bull was standing in the middle of the ring, pawing the ground, eyeing the brilliantly dressed men who strutted in front of him, their capes stretched out at their sides. Looking at the matadors, Elaine could hardly recognise them as the nondescript types who had arrived with the bull that afternoon. Now, in their finery, they were proud, arrogant, very Latin. They looked at the great beast, with its huge horns, contemptuously. They called out to it, trying to make it angry. Suddenly it charged at one, its head lowered, its hooves shaking the ground, the horns lethal weapons.

Elaine gasped and put her hand up to her mouth in horror, but the matador stepped neatly aside, swirling the cloak out of the bull's way. Slowly she lowered her hand, and became fascinated as she saw how skilful the men were, how much it resembled a symbolic kind of dance. She remembered wall-paintings of young people in ancient Greece, both men and women, sporting with bulls, even leaping over them, and she realised that this ritual must be descended from those times, honed over the centuries into a graceful, almost ceremonial dance that was in itself man's defiance against danger and death.

The watchers applauded generously, shouting encouragement, cheering. The bull eventually grew tired, and it was then that the chief matador went up to old Mr Brodey and ceremoniously offered him his cape. Elaine thought it was being given as a keepsake, but Francesca said it was an invitation to take part. Being in his eighties, Mr Brodey had to decline, but did so with such a regretful expression that everyone roared with laughter. Then he waved the matador in Calum's direction!

Expecting that he also would refuse, Elaine was stunned when she saw him get out of his seat, take the cape and move into the centre of the bullring, to the cheers of the crowd. He had changed into white trousers and T-shirt, reminding Elaine vividly of a knight in a fairy-tale as he stood so straight and tall, his hair a golden helmet in the sun. He waved the cape challengingly, and the bull, perhaps excited by seeing someone new, seemed to find a fresh lease of life and immediately charged at

him. Elaine gasped again, but Calum moved swiftly
aside, turning with the bull.

The matadors stood near by, ready to avert any real
danger, but every time the great beast charged at Calum
her heart seemed to stand still in fear. She wanted to
turn away, to leave, but couldn't; she was held there until
the bull had made half a dozen passes, then Calum gave
the cape back to the matador with equal ceremony and
went back to his seat, waving a hand in acknowledge-
ment to the cheers of the watchers.

Afterwards the matadors invited some of the spectators to take part. The young men who had been riding
their motorcycles a couple of hours earlier leapt into the
ring, eager to prove their manhood. One or two of them
weren't quick enough, the matadors having to distract
the bull, but Elaine didn't stay to see. With a muttered
apology to Francesca, she hurried back to the house.

The food was all prepared and being carried out to
the long tables, ready for the end of the bullfight. Barrels
of wine were broached, the meat was taken from the
spits to be carved. Mounds of bread and great dishes of
salad and other foods were put on the tables. Suddenly
everyone was busy again. The spectators ambled down
from the bullring, people pushing to sit at the tables near
their friends, the young men near the prettiest girls.
Francesca managed to avoid Michel and sat next to
Calum. An accordionist began to play, strolling down
between the tables. There was noise and laughter, and
a united determination to have an unforgettable time.

Elaine didn't join in—she was constantly busy, con-
tinuously on the go, mainly inside the house. She was
quite sure that there were far more people here than
they'd invited, but no one seemed to care. More barrels
of wine were tapped, more meat put on the spits, cutlery
and glasses belonging to the house taken out. To someone

with Elaine's efficient, methodical mind, it was a nightmare of a challenge, but one she found that she rather enjoyed in a hair-tearing kind of way. Everyone was so cheerful about it, so laid-back, that it was impossible to worry. And, as everyone seemed to be enjoying themselves hugely, there really wasn't much point.

When all those present had finally eaten enough it was dark. Lamps were lit, coloured bulbs hung in the trees, candles flickered on the tables. A fire-eater, a juggler and a musician entertained. Then the fado dancers came, the old music echoing around the hills as their heels tapped the wooden stage, their colourful costumes swinging.

Elaine paused to look round the kitchen. It was a shambles: piles of crockery stacked everywhere. She was about to order her paid helpers to start clearing it when Calum came in. He said something to the workers in Portuguese that brought great smiles to their faces, and they immediately downed tools and went outside.

'What did you say to them?' Elaine demanded.

'I told them to take a break, to go and watch the dancing.' His eyes went over her. 'And you must too. You haven't eaten, have you?'

She shook her head, surprised that he'd noticed, and Calum found a clean plate and piled it with salad, then poured a glass of wine for her.

'Come on, eat this while you watch the dancers.'

She went with him meekly enough, realising that he was right—she needed a break. He found a space at one of the tables for her and she expected him to leave her then, but instead he sat down beside her and explained what the dances signified, told her which region of the country each one came from. There was still plenty of wine being circulated; Calum refilled her glass a couple of times although she murmured a protest. She felt better

when she'd eaten and didn't attempt to go back inside.
The dancers were resting and a woman was singing, the
haunting melodies drifting into the night air.

'What is she saying?' Elaine asked.

Calum gave a small shrug. 'It's more an expression
of feeling than words. It's the hardness of continually
working to live, the suffering of losing a loved one, the
harshness of war and famine, the lost hopes. All the
sadness of all the years through which the poor people
have been telling their history through these songs, I
suppose.'

'Don't they have any happy songs?'

'Of course, but they dance to those.'

She had seen the fado dancers before, briefly, at the
party in the wine-lodge, but somehow they seemed far
more evocative out here in the open, in the countryside
where the singing and dancing had evolved. There they
had played western music too; here it was all Portuguese.
When the dancing became general, Francesca again
joined in, and Elaine found herself wishing that she could
too. But after the way she'd snubbed Calum last time
he was hardly likely to ask her again. Not that she particularly wanted to dance with him, of course; it was just
that she'd had enough wine to feel relaxed and the music
was getting to her.

'Thanks for the meal.' Standing up, she looked round.
'I think most of my helpers have deserted,' she said
ruefully.

Calum grinned. 'One can hardly blame them. Give it
a while longer and I'll round them up for you.'

'Thanks.'

She went to leave but he said, 'Must you go back?'

'There's the kitchen . . .'

He made an impatient gesture. 'Surely it can wait?'

She hesitated a moment, then sat down again. 'Why did you go into the bullring?' she asked him.

Calum had been watching the dancers, but he turned to give her his full attention. 'Do you disapprove?'

'No. I thought I would, but it was, as Francesca said, like a ballet. But you're not a professional; you could have been hurt.'

He shrugged. 'It was expected of me. I would have lost face if I hadn't.'

'And is that important to you—not losing face?'

She spoke intently and his eyebrows rose a little. 'I haven't really thought about it, but yes, I suppose it is. Although Chris and my other cousin, Lennox, would have done the same. We're Brodeys, you see, and the House of Brodey is very important here. The men work for us and need to respect us; they would hardly do that if I'd refused to face the bull.'

'Why do they *need* to respect you?'

Calum put his elbows on the table, rested his chin on his hands but still kept his eyes on her. 'This is a very deep conversation. Let's see, now... Tell me, are you good at cooking, waiting on table, dealing with people?'

'Yes, I think so.'

'That sounds suitably modest, which means you must be good. And I imagine you turn your hand to anything, if necessary, in an emergency?'

'Yes, of course.'

'The people you employ, that you hire, presumably they know this. And I'm sure they respect you for it and do a better job because they know you have such high standards yourself.'

'Oh, I see what you're getting at. But do you ever work in the vineyards?'

'I did when I was younger. Grandfather made all of us serve our apprenticeship in the fields, and we all did a viniculture course at the university at Vila Real.'

'But it's still necessary to prove your worth against the bull?'

'For a man it is, yes.'

She gave him a contemplative look. 'You were extremely good,' she said, deliberately flattering him.

Calum shrugged. 'Thank you—but the bull was so tired by then that a child could have fought it.' He raised an eyebrow. 'You didn't really think there was any danger, did you?'

'No,' she admitted without prevarication.

'I see.' He gave her an arrested look. 'So it was a test, was it?'

She hesitated for a moment before saying, 'No, of course not.'

But she had left it too long and he knew it was a lie.

'Now, why should you want to test me, I wonder?' Lifting his hand, he touched a loose tendril of her hair. 'They say that all redheads have fiery tempers. Is this true?'

'I don't know any other redheads,' she answered, adding pointedly, 'Do you?'

'No. But I somehow think that you could let your temper rip if you didn't work so hard to control it.'

'Oh, really? What makes you so sure?' Elaine's voice was light but her heart had begun to feel tight in her chest in the strangest way.

Calum smiled slightly and his finger brushed her cheek. 'Your eyes give you away. You might be able to control your features and your tongue, but you can't hide the fire in your eyes. Such beautiful green eyes that spark like rare jewels when you're angry.'

She had been almost holding her breath and looking away, unable to meet his eyes, but now she glanced quickly at him and surprised Calum watching her searchingly. He was flirting with her, she suddenly realised, waiting to see how she would react. Immediately she relaxed, smiled a little crookedly, and said, 'Now who's testing whom? Did I pass your test?'

'Did I pass yours?' he countered.

But she merely smiled enigmatically and quickly got to her feet again. 'Excuse me; I can see someone looking for me.'

Ned Talbot was in fact standing by the door to the house looking round, and she chose to think it was for her. She hurried across and they went into the kitchen.

'We shall have to make a start on this lot,' Elaine said, and looked for an apron to tie round her.

'The housekeeper here speaks English; I'll find her and get her to round up our helpers,' Ned offered.

Elaine didn't wait for him to come back, but set to work standing at the big old sink. There was no dishwasher here so everything would have to be done by hand. Gradually the helpers drifted back, and the kitchen began to look more like a store-room, with stacks of clean crockery growing on every surface. Then there was a terrific explosion outside and the place cleared of helpers again as if by magic.

'What on earth was that?' Elaine exclaimed.

'The fireworks, I think,' Ned answered. He gave her a wistful look. 'I always did enjoy a good firework display.'

Elaine looked at him for a moment, then grinned. 'So do I. Let's go.'

Abandoning the kitchen, they too went out to watch. The fireworks were being let off on the crest of a nearby hill, lighting up the sky for miles around. They

seemed to go on endlessly, great rockets that exploded
into coloured lights brighter than day, balls of fire that
burst into shooting sprays of gold and silver stars, more
colourful than those already in the sky. Pyrotechnics
outdoing nature.

The local guests were watching in rapt admiration, but
Elaine saw Francesca standing to one side, looking a little
bored. Michel went up to her with a drink. She took it
from him and stood with him for a while, but then went
over to join Calum and a couple of other people, leaving
Michel to follow her or not, as he pleased. He did, of
course; Francesca had that magnetic kind of attraction
that would always make men follow her, despite being
snubbed.

It occurred to Elaine that it would take quite a man
to make Francesca happy, to win and keep her love.
Michel certainly wasn't that man, for all his suave charm,
but Calum...? Watching him as he put a casual hand
on Francesca's shoulder, Elaine thought that he could
well be. His character was certainly strong enough, he
had power and wealth, was good-looking, and probably
knew Francesca inside out. Maybe that was what attracted Francesca to him; with Calum she could be
herself, could relax completely, had no need to pretend
to be happy, as Elaine had seen her pretend with other
people sometimes.

Seeing the casual way that Calum touched Francesca
made Elaine wonder again if they were having an affair.
The thought made her chest tighten with a kind of anger
that she recognised as jealousy. It was an emotion it
had grown used to when she was married to Neil and
had found out about his affair, that time she lost her
baby. It surprised her that she should feel it again now,
and for so little reason. All because she found Calum
physically attractive. But then, all the Brodeys were; they

all had a magnetism that was impossible to ignore; even old Mr Brodey still had a warmth and charm that drew people to his side. When he was young he must have been very much like Calum was now, Elaine thought, her eyes still on him.

Perhaps sensing that he was being watched, Calum turned his head and their eyes met. He didn't nod or smile. Instead he began to frown.

Elaine turned her head away, doing it casually, outwardly indifferent but her heart beating rather fast. Fool! Now Calum must surely suspect that she fancied him. Angry with herself, her pleasure in the firework display gone, she nevertheless waited until it had ended before going back to the house. She worked solidly for the next hour, her helpers drifting casually in to do a little work and drifting off again. If she had been paying British workers Elaine would have expected and insisted on a more efficient attitude, but she recognised that for her helpers recruited locally tonight was very special—a day to remember—and so she let them do as they pleased.

The party went on most of the night, some people getting too drunk to leave at all. At about three in the morning Calum came into the kitchen and found Elaine packing glasses into boxes, ready to be collected.

'Elaine! Still working? This surely goes beyond the call of duty.'

She glanced at him, then back at her task as she said, 'Somehow I don't think anyone will be in a fit state to work tomorrow morning—or later this morning, rather.'

'And nor will you. Leave it, please.' Coming over to her, Calum put his hand on her arm.

She didn't think she betrayed the quiver this sent through her, but she had an idea that there wasn't much that Calum missed. 'All right.' She straightened, and moved her hand away, pretending to look at her watch.

'It is late, isn't it? But it was a good party; everyone seemed to enjoy themselves.'

'A lot of them still are,' Calum said with a grin. 'Come and see.'

Most of the families had gone, the children had been dragged home, but there were still a lot of people sitting at the tables, singing as the accordionist played again. Men had their arms round the waists of their wives, and girlfriends leant sleepy heads on their boyfriends' shoulders.

At her own shoulder, Calum said softly, 'I shall be very surprised if we aren't asked to stand as godparents to a clutch of babies because of tonight.'

'Are you often asked to be a godparent?'

'It's the custom,' he explained. 'Especially after a celebration like the bicentennial of the company.'

'Francesca too?'

'Oh, yes. Lots of little girls will be named after her.'

'I thought she looked very relaxed tonight,' Elaine commented. 'She seemed to enjoy watching the fireworks with you.'

Which wasn't exactly true, but Elaine hoped that Calum would think she'd been watching his cousin rather than him.

It seemed to work; he gave her a quick, assessing glance, then said, 'Yes, she always likes it here.'

'I'm not surprised. It's very beautiful, and it has a quality that your house in Oporto doesn't have.'

'What quality?'

'I'm not sure how to describe it. A oneness with nature. A kind of tranquillity, perhaps.' She laughed. 'Although you'd never think that today with all these people. I felt it for a while yesterday, though, before everything started to happen.'

'Yes, it's a good place to come to unwind. I'd like to get here more often, but it's difficult sometimes.'

'I suppose your work must keep you very busy,' she remarked, saying it because it was the expected thing to sympathise with high-powered men like Calum.

But he surprised her by saying, 'No busier than yours does, I imagine. Do you get much time for holidays?'

'Not much, although I've promised myself a week off once your celebrations end. After that the wedding and party season really gets under way and I'll be very busy until September.'

'Where will you go?'

'I haven't really thought about it. Probably collapse at home, I expect.'

'Hardly a get-away-from-it-all holiday.'

Francesca came walking up to them, still looking wide awake, although Michel, behind her, looked rather the worse for wear. 'The party's over, I think. Goodnight, coz.' She kissed Calum on the cheek, then said a casual, 'Goodnight, Michel,' over her shoulder to the Count, before putting an arm through Elaine's. 'Let's walk back to the house together, shall we? I really want to congratulate you. You coped magnificently,' she said as they walked away from the two men.

When they'd gone a few yards, Elaine said wryly, 'It's OK, he isn't following you.'

Francesca laughed. 'Michel is the most tenacious man I've ever met. He hangs on like a limpet. And he seems to think that if I once go to bed with him I'll be his forevermore.'

Elaine hid her surprise, having taken it for granted that Francesca and Michel had been having an affair. 'He fancies himself as a great lover, does he?'

'Don't all men?' Francesca returned with a grimace.

'Yes, I suppose they do—from what I've read.'

'What a diplomatic answer,' Francesca said on a burst of laughter. They reached her room. 'Goodnight, Elaine. Thanks.'

'Oh, I'm always available for escort duty. Goodnight.'

She went to her own room and undressed gratefully, glad that the long day was over. But as she lay in bed she wondered why Francesca had invited Michel to come to Portugal. Had it been to make Calum jealous, to push him into being more than just a cousin? It came to her that she had never met a family like the Brodeys before. They all seemed so vital and attractive, and she was willing to bet that they could be passionate, too, beneath the veneer of mannered politeness. Perhaps the mixture came from being a British family in an exotic setting for so long. Not that she was likely to see the passionate side of their natures, especially Calum's. Unless she made him angry, of course.

Her eyes closed, heavy with fatigue, and she slept soundly, dreamlessly, but woke as a cockerel, which seemed to be right outside her window, lifted its head to act as a natural alarm clock only a few hours later. Elaine stirred, glanced at the real clock and groaned a little. But she knew from experience that once awake she wouldn't go to sleep again. And she felt thirsty from too much wine last night. So, after creeping along to the bathroom for a shower, she dressed, put her hair up, and went in search of some orange juice.

There was no one else around; everywhere was very quiet, the kitchen still untidy. Ignoring it for the moment, Elaine took her glass of juice outside on to the veranda that overlooked the stupendous view. It was a beautiful morning, the sun beginning to climb in the sky and lift the haze of mist that lay along the line of the twisting river. Flowers in the garden shone like bright jewels against the green leaves. Finishing her drink, Elaine leaned forward and put her arms on the balcony rail, closed her eyes and let the soft morning sunlight, warm on her skin, caress her.

She sat there for some time, just drifting, content not to think, and only slowly became aware that she wasn't alone. Opening her eyes, she looked over her shoulder and saw Calum standing by the open door into the house, watching her. She hadn't heard him come out, despite the quiet of the morning.

Smiling a little, he said, 'I feel that I ought to bring you a saucer of very rich cream.'

'Why rich?'

'Only the most beautiful cats get the best cream.' She blinked a little at that, and went to rise, but he said, 'No. Don't say that you've got work to do. Have you seen the winery yet? Let me show it to you.'

She hesitated, but he stood in expectation, waiting for her to join him.

They walked down to the white-painted buildings that were hidden from the house by a fold in the hillside. The doors, painted black but now very weathered, were big and old. Heaving one of them open, Calum took her into the cool, dim interior, the sun's rays laying a path before them. The smell was similar to that of the wine cellars back in Oporto, but here there were huge wooden vats, about six feet in diameter, to take the wine. There were fermentation tanks and crushing machines and strange white dome-shaped little buildings where the wine was mixed with brandy and kept at an even temperature until it was ready to go into casks.

Calum explained the procedure to her as they went round, but Elaine didn't try to take it all in; she was content to get the feel of the place, to let her imagination delight in the process of turning grapes and water into the most delicate of wines. They came to a place with a huge stone trough and Calum said, 'This is where the grapes are trod.'

'You mean used to be trod? Surely nowadays you use those crushing machines you showed me?'

'For most of the grapes, yes.' Calum grinned. 'But we still make a practice of treading the first of the grape harvest. There are people who swear that the only way to get a really outstanding quality wine is by the traditional method.'

'And the treaders—are they the people who were at the party last night?'

'Mostly, yes.'

He was watching her, waiting for her reaction, but if he was expecting her to wrinkle her nose and look disgusted he got a surprise, because Elaine gave a sudden smile and said, 'I imagine they love it. And it seems right somehow that people who've worked to grow the grapes all the year should be involved in the final ceremony that turns the grapes into wine.'

'There aren't many people who think that. Especially women; they tend to think it a disgusting habit and refuse to drink the wine made that way.'

Moving towards the door of the room, Elaine glanced back. 'How unromantic.'

Calum leaned across her to open it, but looked down at her before doing so. She had already moved forward but his arm barred the way. Pausing, she looked up at him. 'Are you a romantic, then?' he asked.

He was very close. She could smell the lingering freshness of his aftershave, see where his hair was still a little damp from the shower, was suddenly deeply aware of her own femininity—and of danger. She forced herself to laugh, although it was rather a brittle sound, and said, 'Romantic? Good heavens, no! I'm a realist. Aren't you?

Doesn't everyone in business have to be nowadays?' And, pushing past him, she went through the door.

'That's a very pessimistic viewpoint,' Calum said as they went out into the sun again. 'Is it impossible, then, do you think, for a businessman or woman to have any idealism, any nostalgia?'

'It might be better for them if they didn't. Then they could concentrate entirely on their work.'

'Is that what you do?' Calum asked, his eyes studying her intently.

Elaine tilted her head to one side, considering. 'I must admit I've spent all my time building up my business over the last three years, yes.'

'To the exclusion of everything else?'

'There hasn't been much time for anything else.'

'So you're living for work, instead of the other way round.'

She frowned, not liking the assumption. 'Everyone who's building up a business has to work hard. Don't you?'

'Yes, of course. But I make a point of taking holidays, of relaxing whenever possible. I let someone else take over and forget it all for a while.'

'You have your cousins to take over from you; I'm on my own.'

'But you must learn to stand aside from it every now and again. People who don't get little enjoyment out of life. They think and talk of nothing but work and become boring to themselves and to others.' Elaine's head started to come up at that but he put a hand on her arm and went on, 'I should hate that to happen to you. Promise me you'll have a real holiday next week. Keep away from England and work. Relax completely.'

She began to shake her head. 'I really don't——'

'But you must.' His hand still on her arm, Calum smiled at her, an assessing look in his grey eyes. 'And I know just the place for you.'

'You do?' Elaine asked in surprise.

'Yes. There's a perfectly simple way for you to get away from it all. You must come here.'

'Here?' She stared at him in stunned astonishment.

'Yes. Why not? You said yourself you found it peaceful here. You'd be able to have a complete rest and recharge your batteries.'

Taken aback, her immediate reaction was to refuse. 'It's very kind of you, of course, but I really couldn't.'

'Are you just being polite or do you really not want to come?' Calum asked bluntly.

Elaine found that she wasn't at all sure. She hadn't expected this, didn't know how to handle it. And most of all she didn't know why Calum had made the offer; was he just being kind again—or was there some other reason? 'I don't know,' she admitted, her heart beating a little fast. 'You've taken me by surprise. Can I think about it?'

'Of course. But I hope you'll accept. The *quinta* is entirely at your disposal for as long as you like.'

Elaine thanked him, bemused by such a generous offer. They walked back to the house and found Chris having breakfast on the balcony. Calum joined him and Elaine went inside to start work. Her helpers weren't so energetic today and it was the afternoon before everything was finished and she could drive back to Oporto with Ned and Malcolm in one of the Brodey company vehicles. The members of the family had gone ahead; a dinner was being given in honour of Mr Brodey and his grandsons by local businessmen in the town that evening, so they had left early with Francesca.

The following day there was a dinner for fellow wine-growers at the *palácio*, but this took little work to organise. It was the following day, when they were holding a grand ball at a hotel in town, that Elaine was again frantically busy, overseeing everything, making sure that the evening went perfectly. The preparations done, she had a meal at the hotel and used a room there to change into a long black evening skirt and beaded top. She would need to go into the ballroom from time to time and must look the part.

The ball went well, although Elaine was surprised to see Tiffany Dean there, escorted by Chris Brodey. Tiffany seemed to be having a wonderful time; she was beautifully dressed, sparkling and vivacious. Curious, Elaine looked at Calum to see how he was taking it, and saw that his mouth was tight with scarcely suppressed anger. Francesca, too, seemed to be annoyed. Strange; if she was in love with Calum she shouldn't care if Tiffany was with someone else. Unless she was so unsure of him that she just didn't want the other girl anywhere near Calum.

Elaine tried to dismiss the Brodeys and their petty jealousies from her mind. But that wasn't so easy to do where Calum was concerned. Especially now that he'd offered her the *quinta* for a holiday. She hadn't made up her mind about that yet. Instinct told her to leave, to sever all ties with the family. If she went on seeing Calum, then this restlessness, this strange sensual excitement, might grow even more than it had already. Because it was impossible now to convince herself that she wasn't attracted to him. Since the party at the *quinta*, almost from the moment she'd seen him stand like a golden god to fight the bull, she had known a sense of need, a longing ache that was hard to fight.

The day after the ball was a comparatively quiet one. There was just a lunch for all the family at the house, before they broke up and went their separate ways. Their work done, Ned and Malcolm took a taxi to the airport, but Elaine stayed on to deal with the heap of paperwork that the week's festivities had engendered. She went methodically through it all, making sure that the bills from all the local companies she had used were correct, paying them, and then making out her own final bill for the Brodey House. It was a huge sum, but she had no doubt that Calum would pay it at once; she had complete faith in his integrity as a businessman. And besides, she'd had the company checked out before she'd undertaken the commission, as she did with all her potential customers.

She could have gone home the following day, and should have done, but Francesca had invited her out for a thank-you dinner, along with Calum, that evening, and Elaine had rather unwisely accepted. Feeling in a holiday mood now that the celebrations were safely and so very successfully over, she went into town and had her hair done, then succumbed to an evening dress that she saw in the window of a boutique. It was a soft, floating affair in shades of green that seemed to do wonders for her eyes and was therefore impossible to resist.

Elaine wore the dress that evening, and let her hair hang almost loose, just taken back from her face. She looked good and knew it, but went across to the main house to join the others for a pre-dinner drink feeling strangely full of nervous tension, like a young girl invited to a grown-up party for the first time. When she walked into the drawing-room she felt a surge of inner gratification at the way Calum's eyes widened when he saw her. He had been saying something to Francesca, but stopped in mid-sentence, his gaze taking Elaine in, almost as if he had never really looked at her before. Which he probably hadn't, Elaine told herself wryly, deliberately bringing herself back to earth. After all, who ever really looked at the caterer?

If she had had an effect on him, Calum only let it show for a moment, then he became his charming, well-mannered self again, fixing Elaine a drink, talking to them both while they drank. Afterwards, he went to get his car and Elaine and Francesca strolled, chatting, into the hall to wait.

'Calum tells me he's offered you the *quinta* for a holiday?' Francesca remarked.

'Yes, it's very kind of him.'

'Will you go?'

'I'm not sure if I can summon up enough courage to abandon my business for another week,' Elaine admitted lightly. 'Although it's extremely tempting. It's such a beautiful place, and so gorgeously peaceful.'

'You should go,' Francesca urged. 'In fact I might join you for a few days.'

Before Elaine could reply to that, a car drew up outside and they went out, thinking it was Calum. But instead they saw that Sam Gallagher, the American, had arrived.

Francesca became very still for a moment, then said to him with biting coldness, 'I should have thought that even someone as insensitive as you would have realised that you're no longer welcome at this house.'

Elaine gasped at her rudeness, but Sam said grimly, as he came towards them, 'I was hoping you'd be here, Princess.'

The two of them looked as if they were all set for a first-class row, but luckily Calum drove round and got out of his car. Francesca tried to pull Elaine towards it, saying, 'We're just going out to dinner,' but Sam stepped in the way, insisting that Francesca have dinner with him instead.

It seemed that Francesca had walked out on him on a lunch date earlier that day and the big American was determined that they go out together now.

Francesca called on Calum to help her, to throw Sam out, but to Elaine's amazement Calum put a hand under her own elbow to propel her into his car, then left the other two still arguing on the steps.

As they drove away Calum burst into laughter. 'Look through the back window,' he told her.

Twisting round, Elaine was just in time to see Sam sling Francesca over his shoulder and stride round the side of the house with her.

'Good heavens!' Elaine exclaimed, then turned back to Calum. 'Shouldn't you go back? You don't know what he might do to her.'

'I'm hoping he'll...' he paused '...give her what she needs.'

'And what do you think she needs?'

'To fall head over heels in love with Sam, of course.'

She stared at him. 'But I thought she disliked him.'

'Maybe she's telling herself that, but he's exactly the right man for her. He has the strength to give her the love she needs and to keep her to heel.'

'I thought Francesca rather—admired—*you*,' Elaine said tentatively, watching his profile.

It merely made Calum give an amazed laugh. 'Me? What on earth gave you that idea? We'd both rather run a mile! No, Francesca is lonely and restless. She'd like to work for the Brodey House, be on a par with Chris and Lennox and I, but Grandfather won't let her. He thinks a woman's place is in the home. And Francesca is the apple of his eye; he spoils her and won't let her do any work.'

'So you think she ought to fall for Sam?'

'Definitely.'

So, one down and one to go, Elaine reflected, thinking
of his interest in Tiffany Dean. The odds now were even,
she thought, rather incoherently, her heart beating fast.
They drew up outside a brightly lit restaurant, but before
they got out Elaine, without giving herself time to think
about it, said in an offhand voice that hid a wave of
excitement, 'Oh, by the way, I've checked with my office
and we're not too busy at the moment, so I will be able
to take you up on your offer of the *quinta* after all.'

CHAPTER FOUR

THE restaurant shouted expensive from the moment they went through the door. Calum was greeted by name and given every attention—too much attention to Elaine's mind: there seemed always to be a waiter hovering near by. They were shown to a discreet table, the place that had been set for Francesca quickly cleared away.

'I'm glad you've decided to accept the *quinta*,' Calum said as soon as they sat down.

Watching carefully for his reaction, Elaine said, 'Francesca said she might come too.'

He looked surprised and she thought he frowned a little. 'Did she? Well, it depends on what happens with Sam, I suppose. Will you still go if she changes her mind?'

'Oh, yes. I'm used to being on my own. It doesn't bother me.'

His eyes came up to study her face. 'Have you been a widow long?'

'Nearly three years.'

'Around the time you started your business, then?'

'Yes. I started it almost immediately.'

'What made you choose catering?'

'I'd organised events for charity, for friends, and enjoyed it. It seemed natural to turn a hobby into a job.'

'I would have described it more as a profession, because that's how you handle it—with great efficiency and professionalism.'

'Thank you.' Elaine was pleased with the compliment because it had been paid to her work, on which she prided herself, and wasn't a personal one.

The waiter came with a bottle of champagne. Calum lifted his glass and said, 'To your continued success, Elaine. And thank you for making our bicentenary such a memorable one. It all went magnificently. My grandfather asked me to add his thanks to mine; he's very grateful for all your efforts.'

'I hope the week hasn't worn him out too much,' she said politely.

'No, he thrived on it. Meeting all the buyers, seeing all his old friends did him a power of good. Hopefully it will give him a new lease of life.'

'You're all very fond of him, aren't you?'

'Yes, especially Lennox and myself. Our parents were all killed together in an accident when we were quite young, so Grandfather brought us up. But he tried to be fair and always invited Francesca and Chris to Portugal for the holidays, so we all know each other very well.'

'Perhaps that's why you're all so much alike.'

Calum's eyebrows rose. 'Do you think so? In what way?'

But Elaine wasn't about to tell him that all four cousins had good looks, charm and strong attractiveness, so she just said, 'Oh, I don't know—something in your manner, perhaps.'

He gave her one of his engaging grins. 'That sounds like a very tactful way of saying that we're all much too proud and arrogant.'

'Do you think you're arrogant, then?' she asked, immediately intrigued.

'So I've been told,' he said wryly. He didn't enlarge on it, just beckoned the waiter with the menus over.

'What would you like to eat? The food here is always extremely good.'

When she'd found that they were to spend the evening alone, Elaine had felt a flair of apprehension as well as the crazy excitement that had led her to accept the *quinta*. Now it came back as she wondered what Calum would make of her sudden acceptance. But they didn't touch on personal subjects while they ate, just chatted generally, Elaine finding Calum a most entertaining and attentive host. She asked him about the wine trade and he told her a lot, but told it in such an interesting way that she wanted to learn more. They got on to music, and found they'd been to see the same operas, heard the same concerts. Although their lives were so different, it seemed that they shared several interests.

The meal over, they lingered over coffee, Calum seeming not at all in a hurry to leave. 'Tell me about yourself,' he invited, almost making it a command.

Elaine hated that kind of question; it always made you feel as if you were supposed to give a verbal c.v. of your life, and that you had to make it terribly interesting so that the person would like and admire you—almost like selling yourself. When it came to selling her company and its services, then Elaine had no problem, but talking about herself was another matter. She had been too long her parents' obedient child, Neil's docile wife, and now a hard-working widow, to think much about what her own character was like deep down. So now she just said lightly, 'Oh, that would be too boring. Tell me about you instead.'

'Oh, no, you don't escape that easily,' Calum said with a smile. 'Come on, you first.'

Her face tightened a little, but then Elaine shrugged and said, 'All right. I grew up. I got married. I was widowed. I started my business. End of story.' She glanced at him. 'I told you it was boring.'

There was a trace of defiance in her tone that brought Calum's eyes to her face. 'How long were you married?' he asked, casually enough.

'Almost seven years.'

His brows rose. 'You must have been incredibly young when you married.'

'Yes. Just nineteen.'

'A child-bride.'

Elaine's mouth twisted sardonically as she thought back to that time. Yes, she had indeed been childlike and innocent then.

Watching her, Calum said, 'Your marriage obviously meant, and still means, a lot to you.'

'Why do you say that?'

'You smiled when you spoke of it.'

'Did I?' She laughed, thinking how wrong he was, but when Calum raised a questioning eyebrow she merely shook her head. 'Have you ever been married?'

He looked surprised. 'No. The right girl has never come along.'

'The right *blonde* girl, you mean?'

Calum groaned. 'So you've heard about that stupid tradition, too, have you?'

'Francesca told me.'

Frowning, suddenly serious, he said harshly, 'I wish it had never begun, never got talked about. That's why Tiffany gatecrashed the garden party, you know; she'd heard about the tradition and thought she'd try her luck. It made me extremely angry. I can't stand lies and deceit.' Frowning, he added, 'I suppose Francesca also told you that Chris and Tiffany are together now; that he's taking her to America with him?'

Elaine's breath caught in her throat. The odds now, it seemed, were all in her favour. She shook her head. 'No, Francesca didn't say anything; I saw them dancing together at your ball. They looked as if they were an item.'

'Chris is a fool,' Calum said shortly. 'Tiffany will be nothing but trouble to whoever she's with; she'll take it with her wherever she goes.'

Elaine thought he was being rather harsh, and wondered if it was because he was disappointed that things hadn't worked out for him with Tiffany, but she was eager now to get his thoughts away from the other girl so she said, 'Will it be all right if I go to the *quinta* tomorrow?'

'Yes, of course. I'll phone the housekeeper first thing and tell her to get a room ready for you. There isn't a pool there, I'm afraid; we always go down to the river to swim.'

'Is it clean enough?'

'Oh, yes, it's all mountain water that far upstream. There are very few towns on the river up to the Spanish border, but there are some beautiful towns in the hills. I'll make sure a car is put at your disposal so that you can explore—just in case Francesca doesn't go with you.'

Elaine's thoughts drifted back to the *palácio*, and the way Sam had swung the sophisticated princess over his shoulder, in true caveman style. Was that why Calum was lingering over the meal? she wondered, suddenly unsure of herself again. To give the other two more time alone at the house? 'Do you really think Francesca and Sam will get together?' she asked.

Calum laughed. 'Either that or they'll have murdered each other by now. Would you like a liqueur?'

'No, thank you.'

'Not even a Brodey port?' he asked with a smile.

She laughed. 'Don't you get tired of drinking it?'

'What a question to ask a Brodey!' Reaching across, he pretended to slap her hand as it lay on the table. There was laughter in his eyes and a warmth that sent tingles down her spine.

Signalling the waiter, he ordered a cognac for himself, which made Elaine laugh in her turn. 'Now who deserves to get his hand slapped?'

'Please don't give me away,' he begged. 'Grandfather would never forgive me.'

He was joking, of course, and Elaine joined in the game. 'I see that I shall now be able to blackmail you. Pay up or I'll tell.'

'And just what do you want?' he asked, looking at her with a smile, his grey eyes amused.

She pretended to consider, but then shrugged. 'I can't think of anything right now—but I will,' she added threateningly.

'So you're going to hold a sword over my head, are you?' He finished his drink and leant forward. His eyes holding hers, he said, 'This has been a most enjoyable evening, Elaine. Thank you.' And, picking up her hand, he kissed her fingers lightly.

Trying very hard not to let the gesture go to her head, Elaine excused herself and went to the cloakroom.

Was she getting excited over nothing? she wondered. Kissing her hand had probably meant little to him: Calum might do it all the time, the way French and Italian men did; it was just part of his Latin upbringing. And just because she was attracted to him, it didn't mean that he felt anything for her, for heaven's sake. He was just being dutifully polite to the caterer who had served the Brodey family well. Because Elaine knew Francesca, Calum had felt it necessary to show his thanks by more than just paying her bill—that was all it was, she told herself fiercely.

But the restless, aching longing was still deep inside her, so strong and so much a stranger that it couldn't just be ignored. Although she ought to ignore it, because no way did she want the complication of a man in her life.

It came to her then, as she held her lipstick to her mouth, that Calum was most unlikely to be a complication. He had to carry on his family's name, its traditions, and there was no way he was going to allow himself to fall in love with a working girl, and a red-headed one at that. No, his destiny was among the rich and aristocratic, the kind of people who hired her services. It was there that he would look for his blonde wife. But that didn't mean that he couldn't meet other women first.

So to have an affair with him would be safe. She could give in freely to this growing need for him, just for a few days, and then go back to England, leaving him here, each of them free to go on with their lives. It would be just a kind of holiday romance. Mediterranean men were fond of those; she'd read it often. Not that Calum was in the usual class, of course, but she supposed it all amounted to the same thing in the end.

Elaine finished putting on her lipstick, stood back, and saw the excitement in her own eyes. She had never had an affair in her life, had never envisaged herself as the kind of woman who would have one. But her body was urging her otherwise, telling her to start living again, and it was a message she was beginning to listen to.

Calum was waiting for her in the foyer, beside him a waiter with her jacket over his arm. But Calum took the jacket from him and helped her on with it himself. It felt cool outside; although the days were getting hotter all the time, the nights were still chilly. It was getting late, almost midnight, Elaine saw from the clock on the car dashboard, although that probably wasn't late by Portuguese standards. She wondered again what had happened between Francesca and Sam. If they had got together then Francesca wouldn't want to come with her to the *quinta*, in which case Calum might come there, if he was really interested in her. But if Francesca had quarrelled with Sam she would probably still want to come with her.

To Elaine it seemed all if, if, if. And she didn't like it. She wanted to be in control of her life, not dependent on other people's whims. As far as her business went, she was in control, and to a certain extent in her personal life; she had learned to say no to her mother-in-law, for instance. But she'd had little experience with men, both before her marriage and since. Things had changed a lot in the decade since she'd become engaged to Neil. It was OK now for a woman to ask a man for a date. It was even OK to tell him she was interested. Elaine's thoughts didn't go further than that, and she wasn't at all sure that she would have the nerve to do it.

But as they turned into the drive leading to the *palácio*, she felt a sudden feeling of desperation, was terrified in case she lost this opportunity, so she said, trying valiantly to keep her voice steady, 'Why don't you take a day off and come up to the *quinta* while I—while Francesca and I are there? Maybe we could go sightseeing together?'

As a way of asking for a date it was a very poor, ambiguous effort, but when Calum pulled up outside the house he turned to look at her with open interest in his eyes. 'Thank you. That sounds a most pleasant idea.' He glanced through the windscreen. 'But Sam's car is still here, so maybe Francesca won't be going with you after all.'

They got out, but Calum didn't take her into the house, instead walking through the courtyard and across to the block in which she had her room.

'I'll arrange for the *quinta* to be ready for you,' he told her. 'And I'll let you know in the morning whether Francesca will be going with you. If she isn't, I'll put a car at your disposal.' Putting his hand on her arm, he drew her to him. 'Goodnight, Elaine.'

'Goodnight. I——' Her words were lost as he bent to kiss her.

It wasn't a long kiss, and he didn't even put his arms round her. It was just his mouth against hers, warm, but almost an experiment. Perhaps it was; perhaps he was testing her clumsy invitation. Whatever, it sent a shock of heat searing through her veins, a shock so intense that it held her still, too overwhelmed to move.

Calum drew back and she opened her eyes to find him watching her. He smiled, said again, lightly, 'Goodnight, Elaine,' and turned to walk away.

Elaine didn't see or hear from Calum the next morning; it was Francesca herself who rang to say that she would be coming to the *quinta* with her. Stifling a great surge of disappointment, Elaine joined her at the car. Francesca looked terrible, as if she hadn't slept at all the previous night, which would have been intriguing except that the Princess's mouth was drawn into a tight line and there was no happiness in her face. It was definitely the face of a sleepless night spent alone rather than in the arms of a lover.

'Would you mind driving?' she asked, and got into the passenger seat before Elaine could reply.

'OK, but yell at me if I go on the wrong side of the road.'

'Aren't you used to driving on the right-hand side?'

'I've never tried it before,' Elaine admitted.

'You'll soon get used to it. Didn't you ever come to Europe for holidays when you were married?'

'Yes, but my husband always drove.'

'You were content to be the passenger, were you?' Francesca said on a slightly scathing note.

'No, but I wasn't given any choice.'

'Oh—I see.' The Princess looked taken aback, but obviously had problems of her own on her mind. When she'd directed Elaine through the town, she put on a pair of dark glasses, leaned back in her seat, and lapsed into silence.

Greatly curious, Elaine would have loved to know what had happened between her and Sam, but didn't attempt to ask. She and Francesca weren't on close enough terms to confide in each other. If it came to that, Elaine wasn't on close enough terms with anyone to confide in them; the hurt and disappointment of her marriage, the shame of it, she kept strictly to herself.

They took a different route today, along a main road that was much straighter and faster than the winding road along the river, and reached the *quinta* in time for a late lunch. Elaine had, of course, already met the housekeeper, Senhora Varosa, when she'd stayed at the *quinta* for the bicentennial party, and the Portuguese woman greeted her with warm smiles. She served their lunch then left them to eat it, going back to her own house, which was near the winery, out of sight.

'Doesn't anyone actually live in this house?' Elaine asked.

'No, but Senhora Varosa's sister will always come and stay if she's needed. Chris's mother—she's an artist, you know—comes here to paint sometimes, and she likes to have someone here with her for company. And when Grandfather comes his chauffeur always sleeps in the house.'

'And you?' Elaine asked.

Francesca shrugged. 'I don't often come here alone, but it doesn't worry me.' She didn't eat a lot, picking at her food, and afterwards said, 'Look, Elaine, I'm sorry to be such boring company, but would you mind if I went to my room to rest? I didn't sleep very well last night.'

'No, of course not. You go ahead. I think I'll take a walk down to the river.'

It was a pretty, if lonely walk. The vines stretched in both directions but near the path wild flowers had come into their own, carpeting the ground with their heads of yellow, white and purple. The track curved ever lower, between almond and olive trees now, with here and there a tethered goat or some sheep cropping the grass. When she reached the river Elaine sat down on a grassy bank, resting her chin on her drawn-up knees. Near by, on the riverbank, there was a wooden boat-house, its doors locked, but otherwise there were only a couple of houses in sight, nestling in the hills across the river. On that side, too, the road meandered along, parallel with the railway line that went all the way to the Spanish border.

The river was wide and looked deep and green. As she sat there a big boat, three decks high, came slowly round the far bend towards her. It was painted white but looked as if it had seen better days—rather old-fashioned in shape and with scrape marks along the sides. On its upper deck, out in the sun or under an awning, there was a litter of tourists in plastic chairs. A train coming along the railway line gave out a hoot and the boat's siren gave an answering friendly call in return. It made Elaine smile, and she wondered if the two so different means of transport passed each other regularly like this. Someone on the deck of the ship waved to her, and she waved back. Then it went round the next bend and all was quiet and empty again.

The little incident made her feel philosophical, made her think about her own life. Would Calum come to the *quinta* now that Francesca was here? She didn't think so. And if he did she very much doubted that he would carry on from where that kiss last night had left off with someone else around. She knew instinctively that Calum would be too circumspect for that, too private a person to display his feelings so openly. If he had any feelings for her. Maybe last night he had just thought it the gentlemanly thing to do to follow up the lead she'd given him.

Away from his disturbing presence now, able to think more clearly, Elaine began to wonder if Francesca's being here with her might be a good thing after all. Maybe it was even fate. Maybe she just wasn't destined to have an affair with Calum, or anyone else. And even if Calum did come it wasn't too late to draw back. After all, it had only been a kiss. A kiss could be laughed off, didn't have to lead anywhere.

It was easy enough to tell herself that, sitting there in the sunlight, but the truth was that she'd been quite devastated by her own reaction to it. Her libido, so long killed off by Neil's selfish lovemaking, had sprung achingly to life—and longed for more of the same.

Her mind strongly advised caution, but her body craved sexual fulfilment just for once in its life. And her heart, her feelings? They, poor things, didn't know whether they were coming or going.

The two girls spent a pleasant evening together, preparing their own meal, talking about books, schooldays, avoiding the subject of men. Francesca didn't look as if she'd rested much, and they were both glad to go to bed early, each of them with her own problems to think about.

The next day, Friday, they drove to Regua early in the morning and caught the little train that followed the course of a tributary of the river, winding its way up the sides of the mountains, stopping at tiny stations that were no more than a platform jutting out from the steep hillsides. People piled into the train on their way to work or school, most of them young, all of them short and dark-haired, but with big brown eyes and good-looking faces.

They came to Vila Real, the town where Calum had attended the university, and wandered round, Elaine buying an attractive basket from a shop where the wares spilled out on to the pavement. They had lunch at a small café, eating delicious omelettes washed down with the dry white wine of the region, then caught a bus back to Regua, holding tightly to the seat in front as the bus swayed down the hillsides into the valley.

It was a good day, one that they both enjoyed. Again they cooked themselves a meal in the evening and afterwards took a bottle of wine into the sitting-room. It wasn't as warm here in the hills as it was on the coast, so Francesca lit the open fire, feeding it with old wood from the vines. They both sat on the floor, leaning back against the chairs, drinking the wine, not bothering to turn on the light. Companionable. At ease.

'I suppose you're wondering what happened with Sam,' Francesca said at length.

'You really don't have to tell me.'

'No, I know.' Francesca paused, then said, 'He's gone back to America.'

'Oh?'

'He wanted me to go with him, but I wouldn't.'

Elaine didn't say anything, letting Francesca take her time, tell only what she wanted to tell.

Strain sounding in her voice, the Princess went on, 'He wanted me to go and see what his life there was like. He wanted me to marry him, to settle down on some cattle-ranch!'

'A cattle-ranch?' Elaine looked startled.

'Yes. Can you imagine it? Me? Rounding up cattle or something? He had a nerve even asking me. OK, the guy turns me on. Turns me on a lot. But marriage!'

'It's a big step,' Elaine agreed. 'Especially if you've been married once and it didn't work out.'

'Quite. I certainly don't want to be caught in that trap again.' Glancing at Elaine, Francesca suddenly remembered. 'Oh, I'm sorry. You probably think it's terrible of me to talk of marriage like that after yours was so happy.'

'Of course not.'

'It's just that I'm such a coward, I suppose. I'm afraid to commit myself again.'

'I don't think you're a coward. As a matter of fact I think you're very brave. Not everyone has the courage to get out of a bad marriage. They just go on taking it, forever hoping that things will change, afraid to make a decision to leave, always believing that it's something in *them* that's made the husband like he is.'

She spoke so vehemently that it was impossible for Francesca not to realise she was talking about herself. 'Oh, Elaine, I'm so sorry. I didn't know.'

'No. Well…I'm the coward, Francesca. If Neil hadn't died I'd probably still be his doormat, still wondering what I'd done, what was so wrong with me that he needed other women.'

'Oh, I see. He was like that.'

'Yes. Wasn't yours?'

'Oh, no. He was quite content to be cruel to one woman at a time.'

For several minutes they were both silent, then Francesca suddenly leaned forward and clinked her glass against Elaine's. 'Well, now we're both free, so let's drink to it. Who needs marriage?'

Elaine's eyebrows rose. 'I notice you say marriage, not men. But nowadays a woman can live her life without a man in it, of course.'

'Of course,' Francesca agreed, but there was a wistful look in her eyes. 'Although one, just now and again, wouldn't come amiss.'

Elaine grinned. 'Someone who turns you on, you mean? Someone like Sam?'

'Sam?' Francesca seemed to give herself a mental shake. 'Oh, Sam was only a momentary aberration. He's completely out of my life. I hope to be a career woman, like you. Calum's promised to find me something to do. I hope he does; I really need to occupy my time. This last week or so has been fun, it's been so busy. But now that all the celebrations are over the time will start to go slowly again.'

'Can't you get a job?'

'I haven't been trained for anything,' Francesca said with a shrug. 'I quit college before I got a degree. Then I just went to loads of parties and that kind of thing until I married Paolo.' She gave a short laugh. 'I've really wasted my life, haven't I?'

'You're still young, Francesca. You could go back to college. Do anything. Be anything you want to be.'

'But that's just it,' Francesca sighed. 'I don't *know* what I want. I still feel so unsettled, so uncertain of anything. I really wish I were more like you.'

The phone rang and she got up to answer it, rising with all the grace of a beautiful cat. When she came back she sat on the floor again, saying, 'That was Calum. He's decided to come down here and spend the weekend with us. Isn't that great? That is the one really good thing in my life: Calum and Chris and Lennox. It's rather like having three wonderful brothers to take care of me.'

They talked for a while longer and then went to bed, each of them looking forward to Calum's arrival, but with very different feelings.

He arrived quite early the next morning, casually dressed, looking relaxed. He greeted both girls with a kiss on the cheek, and to Elaine it was impossible to tell whether or not his smile for her was warmer than the one he gave Francesca.

'I thought we'd take a picnic and go out on the boat as it's such a fine day,' he told them. 'I'll go and get it ready while you put some food together.'

They ran to obey him, both of them filled with the sense of purpose that Calum seemed to bring with him. The picnic prepared, they put on shorts and T-shirts, and carried the hamper between them down to the river. The doors to the wooden boat-house were open and Calum was already aboard a smart motor-boat, the canopy down.

After helping them on to the boat, Calum said, 'Have you any experience of boating, Elaine?'

'Not really.'

'OK, then Francesca can crew and you can be the passenger.'

It was wonderful on the river, so quiet, and yet so much natural life. There were birds and butterflies, wild ducks, and small creatures that scurried into their holes in the riverbank as the boat went cruising by, its engine idling slowly along. They came to a huge dam and went through the lock—it was over thirty metres deep, Calum said, the deepest in Europe. The concrete sides towered over them, and from the bridge above rows of tiny heads looked over the parapet and watched as their boat, minute in the great lock, rose slowly higher and higher. There was a strong smell of dampness and river water, and it felt chill because the sunlight couldn't penetrate that far down, so that it was like rising from hell into heaven as they came up into the light.

Elaine shivered, overawed by the great engineering feat of the dam, but glad to get back on to the river again. They moored above the dam and had their picnic, the conversation light, always fun, both Calum and Francesca making sure that they didn't touch on any subject that excluded Elaine. She felt equal to them, on the same wavelength, and able to converse on the same level. They listened to her opinions, Calum once nodding and saying, 'Yes, you're right, of course; I should have taken that into account.'

Neil would never have done such a thing in a million years: he'd always insisted that he was right and had allowed Elaine to have no views of her own, so that during her marriage she'd several times found herself making the typical doormat remark, 'My husband says...' Now, to have her opinions respected was almost as heady as the physical attraction she felt for Calum.

After lunch they took a walk up a track that led up a steep hillside. There seemed to be every kind of wild flower: heather, bracken, rock cacti, prickly pears, and everywhere wild honeysuckle that twined up trees and over bushes, hanging heavy with scent and the buzzing of honey-bees.

They reached a clearing where the dirt road ended. 'This is the pilgrim's way,' Calum told her, pointing to a path that went up through the trees. He led the way forward and they came to a small shrine of brick, plastered over and painted white. Through the grilled window they could see into the dark interior and made out a statue of the Madonna and Child, with lots of flowers, real and artificial, at its feet. The path went on, winding steeply up the hillside among the trees, reaching at intervals more shrines, similar to the first. Some were grander and also had statues of saints, but all had flowers.

'People come here once a year,' Francesca explained. 'It's a religious ritual that has been going on for centuries. Some even crawl up on their knees.'

It was very steep and the day was hot. Elaine began to pant a little. Calum was ahead of her, but he waited and gave her his hand to help her along. Francesca glanced back, but made no comment.

They reached the top at last, and came out of the trees to a most marvellous viewpoint over the river and the hills, the dam looking like a toy below them.

Calum had let go of Elaine's hand when they'd reached the top, but when she went to lean forward to get a better view he caught her arm. 'Careful. You might feel dizzy.'

Francesca, obviously having seen the view before and with other things on her mind, had gone to sit against a tree, her eyes closed, so they were momentarily alone.

Calum watched her for a moment, then, as if he had read Francesca's mind, he said quietly, 'Did she tell you what had happened between her and Sam?'

Elaine shook her head, unwilling to betray a confidence. 'Just that Sam had gone back to America.'

Calum shook his head. 'I think she made a big mistake, sending him away.'

He frowned, a brooding look in his eyes, and she said, 'Can't you do anything?'

'Such as?'

'Invite him over again.'

'Francesca wouldn't agree to it.'

'So don't tell her.'

Calum's eyes widened and he laughed. 'You're asking me to be devious?'

'All men are devious.'

Maybe there had been a bitter note in her voice, because his eyes became intent on her face for a moment before he nodded and said, 'It's certainly an idea. I'll give it some thought.'

They rejoined Francesca and presently they walked back down the hill, walking in line with Calum in the middle. When they got back to the boat they cruised upriver for an hour or so, then turned and went back through the dam and then home.

To Elaine's surprise, Calum joined them in the kitchen that evening as they prepared the meal, proving to be quite an efficient cook. He caught her look of astonishment and raised his eyebrows. 'What's the matter?'

'I didn't think you were the type who could cook,' she confessed.

'Anyone who's a student for any length of time learns to look after himself. And as I dislike ready-meals and frozen stuff I had to buy a cookbook and teach myself,' Calum told her.

They had a pleasant evening, lingering over the meal, and then playing poker for peanuts, only Francesca kept forgetting and ate her 'money', so that she was soon cleaned out.

The Princess yawned and rose. 'I'm tired. I think I'll go to bed.'

'I can't stand poor losers,' Calum remarked.

He ducked as his cousin took a mock-punch at him, then said, 'I'll help you clear up. No, you sit still, Elaine,' as Francesca went to collect the glasses and things they'd been using.

He followed Francesca into the kitchen and Elaine heard the murmur of their voices for a few minutes but not their actual words. Then Francesca put her head round the door to say goodnight.

When Calum came in Elaine got to her feet and said, 'I'll say goodnight too.'

'No. Stay and keep me company.' And, taking her hand, he pulled her down beside him on the settee.

Her heart leapt but Elaine felt overwhelmingly nervous, like a teenager all over again. Breathlessly, she realised that Calum was not only willing but obviously determined to go on from where that kiss had led. It was time to make up her mind, to stop this here and now, or—or to... She pushed the thought out of her mind, afraid that he would see.

Calum put an arm along the back of the settee, moved nearer, and Elaine hastily said, 'It's so kind of you to let me stay here. It's beautifully quiet, just like you— you said.' Her voice faltered as Calum dropped his arm and put it round her shoulders. 'And the scenery is magnificent. And thank you for taking us to the dam and the——' Calum put his free hand on her face, brushing it with the backs of his fingers '—the lock. I've really never seen anything so——'

'Elaine.'

'Yes.'

'Shut up.' And, putting a hand behind her head, he drew her to him and kissed her.

Again she was overwhelmed, but this time not so surprised by the effect his kiss had on her. Closing her eyes, she lay back against his hand and let herself drown in it, her mind, the world, whirling around her. It was as if life and heat coursed through her veins after she'd been frozen for a very long time. But again she couldn't move, could only be still as he gave her this kiss of life.

His lips drew back and she was immediately filled with a great sense of loss. Reluctantly she opened her eyes to find Calum looking at her with a quizzical, slightly amused look in his eyes.

'It's—er—usual for the lady to reciprocate, you know.' Elaine blushed, and his eyes widened. 'Elaine?' He said her name on a questioning note, his arrested gaze on her face, but then, as if drawn by a magnet, he bent to kiss her again.

She was able after a few moments to lift her hands, shaking though they were, and put them on his shoulders. Immediately his kiss became deeper, creating an even greater flame within her. She clung to him, letting him open her mouth, completely oblivious to everything but the dominance of his lips.

His hand moved down from her neck, trailed across her breast above the silk of her blouse, his fingertips so feather-light that at first she didn't feel it. But then his hand went to the opening and slid inside. She felt it then all right: his fingers seemed like points of flame against her skin. She gasped, made a wild movement and drew her mouth from his. There was heavy-lidded desire in his eyes; they were dark and hungry with it. Suddenly she felt afraid and jerked away from him, would have got to her feet if he hadn't caught her hand.

'What is it?'

She couldn't confess to her own fear. 'F-Francesca,' she stammered.

'She won't come in.' He leaned towards her again.

'No.'

He gave her a questioning look. 'Shall we go to——?'

'No!' she said again, more violently this time, and stood up, shaking off his hand. 'I—I——' She bit her lips. 'Goodnight.' And she hurried to her own room.

There was no lock on the door; for a long time she was afraid that he would follow her, but he didn't. Her room was next to Francesca's; perhaps that was why. Her heart was beating very fast and she was terrified by the heat and need that his kisses had aroused. Had he intended to take her there, on the sitting-room floor, or in his own room? She couldn't! She just wasn't ready for that. It was all right imagining Calum becoming her lover, but when it came to reality she had become frightened by the force of her own desire.

She undressed slowly, her ears alert for any footfall in the now silent house. It took a long while for her heart to quieten, for her to start wondering what on earth Calum had made of her abrupt departure. He would probably go home tomorrow in disgust, she thought wretchedly. He certainly wouldn't be interested in her now.

Elaine fell asleep to that dismal thought, and woke late the next morning. She dressed in a shirt and faded jeans, brushed her hair back and fastened it with a clip, didn't even bother to put on any make-up, and came out of her room sure that Calum would have gone. The house was quiet, seemed empty—until she went out on the veranda and found Calum sitting there, reading, his feet up on another chair. He looked up when she came out but didn't get to his feet. His eyes were on her face, watching her intently.

Licking lips gone suddenly dry, Elaine said, 'Where's Francesca?'

'Grandfather telephoned to say he needed her. She's gone back to Oporto. You and I are alone here.'

CHAPTER FIVE

ALL Elaine could find to say was, 'Oh,' and that on an extremely hollow note.

Putting down the paper he was reading, Calum said, 'I expect you'd like some coffee. There's plenty in the pot.'

Slowly she sat in the chair to his right, pulled it out a little from the table so that her leg wouldn't touch his.

'You take your coffee black, don't you? And with one sugar, I seem to remember.'

'Yes. Thanks.' She sipped her coffee, looking out at the view. A thought occurred to her and she said, an accusation in her mind, 'I didn't hear the phone ring.'

'No, nor did I,' Calum said easily. 'I must have been asleep. I took a while to go off last night, and slept rather late.' He gave her a deliberate look. 'Like you.'

Elaine quickly looked away, unable to meet his eyes. 'Didn't she say goodbye to you?'

'No. I found a note in the kitchen.'

'Oh, I see.'

He didn't attempt to show her the note, and she wasn't at all sure that there really had been one, or a phone call. But she was quite sure that Calum was perfectly capable of sending Francesca away so that he could be alone with her. Especially after she had used Francesca as an excuse to cut short their lovemaking last night. The thought was both unnerving and exciting.

Finishing her coffee, she put the cup down on the table, and Calum immediately reached out and covered her hand. It fluttered under his, but he held her still as he said, 'Would you rather not be here with me, Elaine?'

Now was her chance; all she had to say was no, and he would leave. The tension, the indecisiveness would be gone. But so would the sexual excitement. If he left she could just relax and enjoy the rest of her holiday. But would she enjoy it, knowing that she had thrown away the chance to come alive again? If she said no, she would never see him again. Looking into his face, she thought that it would be a great loss never to see him again.

She took such a long time to answer that his brows rose questioningly, and in the end she was honest with both him and with herself. 'I—I'm sorry, but I just don't know.'

Something flickered in Calum's eyes and he gave a wry smile. 'How old are you, Elaine? Twenty-eight? Twenty-nine?'

She flushed. 'I know what you're going to say—that I'm old enough to know my own mind. But I'm too young and I'm too old, both at the same time.'

'What does that mean?'

But she shook her head, unable to tell him that she was too inexperienced to be able to cope easily with a casual affair, and yet mature enough to know that this could never be anything else, and she mustn't let herself be carried away by the emotions he stirred in her.

Calum went on looking at her for a moment, then came to a decision. 'Let's go and do that sightseeing you invited me here to do.'

A flood of relief ran through her and Elaine gave him a brilliant smile. 'I'll be ready in five minutes.'

She ran inside to change and didn't notice the effect her smile had had on him. Calum sat gazing after her for a long moment, then gave a puzzled shake of his head before locking the house and going out to the car to wait for her.

They went a long way, stopping at a café in a small town for lunch, then driving on through miles of beautiful scenery, past the area where the vines grew, into more arable land with here and there an ancient town with its crumbling castle perched on top of a hill. A few miles from the Spanish border they reached the town of Almeida and drove through the tunnel of the fortified walls into the town. From outside it looked like a massive fortress with high stone walls topped by gun emplacements at every angle: huge, impregnable. Inside it was a quaint old town with cobbled streets between pretty houses, with squares thick with trees and flowers, with leisured people chatting in their doorways or outside the little shops.

Elaine exclaimed in astonishment, 'How on earth did it get like this?'

'The town got fed up with being captured first by one side then the other in the Napoleonic wars,' Calum told her. 'So they built these huge walls to protect themselves.'

'And then they were safe forevermore.'

'Unfortunately, no. They were being besieged by the French when a cannon shot went straight into their armoury and killed a couple of hundred soldiers, so the French took the town yet again. But eventually Wellington recaptured it for Portugal.'

There was a pretty pony-cart, bedecked with ribbons, waiting for passengers by the square. Calum suggested a ride and they climbed into it, but the trap was small and he had to put his arm round her to make more room. He was wearing shorts, she a short denim skirt, so this time their knees couldn't help but touch. Elaine's mouth went dry and she was immediately tense, but Calum seemed quite relaxed, translating the driver's comments about the places they were passing for her.

They drove right up on to one of the big gun emplacements and Elaine could see the plain, in which the fort and its great earthworks stood on a rise, all around her. Then they were in the town again with its rows of little white houses with red pantiled roofs, trotting past the church and the graveyard with tall dark columns of cypresses guarding it, and pulling up outside the little museum situated deep inside one of the gun-towers.

It was cool inside, and they passed a pleasant hour looking at old uniforms, at pictures and descriptions of the battles fought here, at ancient cannonballs and the pathetic relics of men who had lived and died within these dark walls.

Elaine suddenly shivered, and Calum said, 'You're cold. Let's go outside.' He put his hand on her arm, rubbed it gently, then took her hand as they walked out into the sunlight.

They had coffee and cakes at a little pastry shop and set off back to the *quinta*, watching the sun set on the horizon. Somewhere along the road they stopped at yet another town and walked around until they found a little restaurant where music was playing and had a meal. The place had a great atmosphere and they didn't hurry over the meal, joining in the singing with all the other customers, even though Elaine didn't know the words. It was warm and relaxing and fun. Elaine greatly enjoyed herself until it was time to leave and go back to the house.

It instantly felt cold as they came out into the street. The sky had clouded over and all the warmth seemed to have been sucked from the day. She shivered and pulled her jacket round her, walking fast beside Calum as they made their way back to the car park. Immediately they got in the car she became tense again, not knowing what

Calum intended, whether he intended anything at all after her silly confession this morning. She became silent, her eyes fixed out of the window although there was little to see in the darkness. When Calum drove through the gates and drew up outside the house, she could find nothing to say.

They went inside, into the sitting-room where Calum turned on a couple of lamps, then said, 'Would you like a nightcap?'

'I—no, I don't think so, thank you.'

She took off her jacket and went to move towards her own room, but Calum caught her hand. 'Wait. Won't you let me say goodnight?'

'Calum, I——'

'Hush.' He put his finger over her lips. 'I just want to kiss you.' Putting his arm round her waist, he drew her to him. Feeling the tension in her, he said soothingly, 'Relax, my sweet Elaine.' His lips brushed her neck, soft, sensuous. 'Thank you for today,' he murmured. His lips pulled at her earlobe and a great *frisson* of awareness ran through her. Then they moved on to trace the outline of her jaw and chin in tiny little kisses which were hardly more than a touch.

She expected him to kiss her mouth then, wanted him to, but his lips moved to her eyelids, her temples, drifted down her cheek. The tip of his tongue found the corner of her mouth, made her draw in her breath as he toyed with it, slipping inside and then out again. Elaine was standing still, just experiencing the delight of what he was doing, but her hands were drawn up in front of her, palms against his chest, ready to push him away at any moment.

But she didn't push him away, not when he took her mouth at last, sending her senses down into that giddy whirlpool which seemed as if it would never end. Not when his arms went round her and he held her close, arching her against him, letting her feel his dominant manhood, his awakening need for her. Not when his kiss deepened into passion, his shoulders hunching and his hand coming up to cup her breast.

It was when his hand slid down past her waist and her hips to the bare skin at the top of her leg that she froze completely and let out a sound of protest against his mouth.

'Elaine?' He said her name, his voice thicker now, said it on a questioning note.

'You—you said you just wanted to kiss me.'

He sighed and straightened up, pushed his hair back from his forehead. She was watching him uncertainly, but he gave a rueful smile. 'Did I? What a fool I was.' Letting her go, he went over to the drinks tray and poured out two gin and tonics, handing one to her. 'Here. Come and sit down.' Going to the settee, he sat and looked at her expectantly.

After hesitating a moment, she sat down, a space between them. Calum immediately moved up and put his arm round her.

'Want to talk about it?' he asked.

She knew full well what he meant but played for time by saying, 'What about?'

'The reason for your—indecisiveness.'

'I hardly know you,' she prevaricated.

'Oh, Elaine.' He shook his head at her. 'Don't hide behind a weak excuse like that.'

Cornered, she felt a flash of anger. 'It's true, though.'

'Perhaps. But you're old enough to know when you like someone enough and when you don't. And you wouldn't have invited me to come up here if you hadn't been—interested. Isn't that true?' He ran his finger down her cheek, tilted her chin so that she had to look at him.

She nodded reluctantly. 'Yes.'

'So what happened?' She didn't answer and he said, 'Maybe I already know.' Her eyes flew to his at that, wondering if Francesca had said anything to him, but Calum went on, 'I know that widows are often thought of as easy game, that men try to take advantage of them.'

'How do you know?'

He shrugged. 'One hears men talk. Have you experienced it?'

'Yes,' she said bitterly. 'Neil, my husband, was in the army. After he died several of his so-called brother officers came round to offer their sympathy and their help—and they all seemed to think I should have been grateful for a certain kind of "help". They were extremely put out when I told them to get lost.'

'Good for you,' Calum said approvingly.

Studying his face, she said, 'A couple of them were really crude. They came right out and said that because they thought I'd been having sex regularly I wouldn't be able to manage without it, and they were willing to oblige.' She gave a bitter laugh, remembering.

A frown had come into Calum's brows; he looked as if he was going to ask her something, but then changed his mind and said, 'A very hurtful and unsympathetic attitude. But some men, I know, think that's the only way to console a widow.' He paused, then said deliberately, 'Do you think I'm like that?'

'You?' Her surprise was quite obviously genuine. 'No, of course not. Why on earth should I?'

'I thought it might be the reason for your indecision.' His hand went to her hair and toyed with a loose strand, curling it round his finger. 'When I offered you the *quinta*, I must admit that it had crossed my mind to visit you here, but I didn't want to take advantage of you.

So I was pleased when you suggested it yourself. I felt that the instigation had to come from you.'

'Oh.' A thought occurred to her. 'Did you send Francesca away?'

A boyishly mischievous look came into Calum's grey eyes. 'Well, I didn't order her, of course, but I did sort of suggest that three's a crowd.'

It was very flattering to be told that, but even so Elaine said remonstratingly, 'You shouldn't have done that. Francesca was feeling very down; she wanted company.'

'If she feels lonely, then she might start missing Sam.' Leaning forward, he kissed her throat. 'Your skin is as smooth as silk,' he murmured softly. Still kissing her, he said in her ear, 'So why, Elaine, my lovely one?'

She had closed her eyes but now she opened them, knowing he wasn't to be put off any longer. But she couldn't tell him the truth, couldn't denigrate herself in his eyes by telling him how she'd been used—and abused. The shame and humiliation she'd felt then was still there, even after three years. No, there was no way she could tell Calum these innermost truths. After this week she would never see him again; he would become a stranger, and she didn't want a stranger to know her secrets. So she said, 'It's been so long. I feel so—so uncertain.'

He was still for only a moment before saying, 'There's been no one else since your husband?'

'No.' That she could say with complete certainty.

'Then I suppose it's natural that you should feel nervous.' His hand stroked her bare arm. 'Could it be that you also feel, perhaps even subconsciously, that it would be disloyal to your husband's memory?'

She stared at him for a moment, then turned away and leant back against the settee. That was an entirely new thought and held her silent. After finding out about Neil's infidelity she had been so angry that she could think of him only with bitterness and rage. And she still did, when she thought of him at all; mostly she tried to push him out of her mind, and her work had helped a lot with that. But did she still have deep-down feelings of loyalty to the vows that she had made on her wedding-day? No, Neil had broken them constantly, so why should she even think of them now, when he had been dead for so long? That marriage was over, dead and done with.

But the fear that Neil had implanted in her was still there, no matter how desperately she told herself it wasn't so, it hadn't been her fault. The fear of her own inability to please, that Calum would be disappointed in her and show it, as Neil had done. And she was afraid, too, that it would be the same. That all men were the same. That her body would be used for his quick pleasure and her pain. She was terrified that it would be just another animal act, that the sexual arousal of her body would betray her yet again, and that she would hate men and sex forevermore.

Calum was waiting for her to speak. She turned her head to look at him and, summoning all her courage, she said unsteadily, 'No—it wouldn't be disloyal.'

Emotion flared in his eyes and his hand tightened a little on her arm. Holding her gaze, he leaned nearer and said on a husky note, 'So, my darling Elaine, may I do more than just kiss you?'

She knew that she could say no, that he wouldn't coerce her or take her against her will. He had been and was being very patient with her, letting her make the running, state the terms, and she knew he would take her denial like the gentleman he was. And perhaps it was this knowledge that gave her the added courage to say a very tremulous, 'Yes.'

He smiled a little, took the glass she was still holding from her and put it aside. Although he'd asked for per-

mission, Calum didn't do more than kiss her at first.
But the kisses were deep and grew passionate. Elaine
found herself responding to them almost hungrily, experiencing the now familiar feeling of losing herself in
his embrace. A great tremor of awakened sensuality went
through her, and it was only then that Calum's hand
went to the buttons of her shirt, undid them, and pulled
it apart. The catch of her bra seemed to melt at his touch,
and then his hand was on her breasts, caressing, stroking,
wonderful and yet terrible, making her tremble with both
desire and fear.

'You're beautiful,' he breathed as he looked at her.
'So beautiful.'

Bending his head, he kissed her tiny pink nipples, the
bud-like flowers already aroused and proud. Elaine drew
in her breath sharply, her body quivering. Her hands
went to his shoulders, gripped tightly. His lips and then
his tongue explored her, sometimes with a touch that
was feather-light, setting every nerve-end aflame, sometimes with a more demanding movement of his lips that
made her moan aloud. The fear began to leave her, momentarily lost beneath the growing yearning of her body,
beneath these wonderful, voluptuous sensations he
aroused in her. He seemed to know exactly what to do,
where to touch her to excite her, to drive her crazy with
desire.

It was at that moment, exactly as that thought came
into her head, that Calum drew back and stood up,
pulling her up with him. His eyes were dark with charged
desire, intent and hungry. It was a look she had seen in
Neil's eyes too, long ago. 'I want you, my sweet,' Calum
said thickly. 'Let's go to my room.'

'Your—your room?'

'The bed's bigger,' he smiled, and completely mis-
understood the quiver that he felt run through her.

She reached to kiss him, urgently seeking the need she had felt just a moment ago, but she kept thinking how experienced he must be, that he must have been to bed with scores of women. And she was sure now that he would be appalled by her lack of sophistication. He would expect her to do the things that Neil had made her do and which she'd hated, intimate things that in her mind were associated with prostitutes and mistresses. Well, that was what she would be, wouldn't it? But she couldn't think of herself as that, and kissed him with a desperate kind of urgency to regain desire.

It didn't come, but Calum, mistaking her urgency for passion, picked her up and carried her to his bedroom. He set her down inside it and his eager hands went to her clothes, but she pulled quickly away from him, holding her shirt together.

'No! Please, I——'

'You want me to leave you alone for a while?'

'Yes. Yes, I do.'

'All right.' He kissed her hungrily. 'Five minutes.'

He left her and for a moment she leant against the wall, feeling weak and overwhelmed. She must tell him that she'd changed her mind, that she couldn't go through with it, then pack and leave.

For a moment she was filled with the most wonderful sense of relief, but the next knew that it would be no use. For her own future, if it wasn't to be filled with fear and the biggest inferiority complex on record, she had to go through with this. She had to find out for herself whether or not all men were the same. If they were, then she could forget them; they would never be a part of her life. But if it was true that love could be wonderful—and Calum had been so gentle up to now—then a miracle would have happened and her life would be whole again.

Knowing, without any doubt, that she had to go through with it, Elaine went to her own room, found her prettiest nightdress and changed into it, slapped on some scent, and went back to his room to wait for him.

Calum followed her in almost immediately. There was just one lamp burning and she was standing in its light, her figure slim and lovely. As he came into the room, his eyes lingered on her before he came to kiss her. 'I wanted to undress you myself,' he said softly. Then he smiled and reached up to take the clips from her hair. 'Don't you ever let your hair down, ma'am?' he said teasingly.

It fell forward, a thick mane of springing waves that framed her face like a halo of beaten copper. Calum drew in his breath. 'God, you're beautiful.'

Her hair seemed to fascinate him; he touched it caressingly, letting the springing curls twist over his fingers, but then his eyes darkened and he drew her to him and kissed her, his mouth demanding now. As he kissed her he lowered his hands, let them run over her, his touch erotic even through the silk of her nightdress.

Almost automatically Elaine put her hands on his shoulders, but they were balled into tight fists of tension, her nails digging into her flesh. He continued to caress and stroke her hips, her thighs, then caught at the material of the nightgown and began to pull it up. As he raised it with one hand, so the other explored her, his touch on her bare skin sending shock-waves of awareness through her, making her gasp against his mouth, but also making her stiffen nervously.

The silk glided over her skin as if reluctant to leave it as Calum lifted the nightdress over her head. He threw it aside and took a step back so that he could look at her. Elaine turned her head away, unable to meet his gaze, her body becoming rigid with apprehension.

Reaching out, Calum cupped her tip-tilted breasts. 'Your body is perfect,' he said softly. 'So lovely.'

She closed her eyes, grateful for his compliments, but they weren't enough to dispel the fears. He bent to kiss her body, letting his lips, his fingers explore her at will. He kissed her gently, tenderly, in places that sent her senses reeling, that brought a flush of colour to her skin. Tremor after tremor ran through her, but her fists were still balled at her sides and her teeth clamped together.

Rising, Calum kissed her mouth. 'Relax,' he said softly. 'Relax, my sweet.'

She tried very hard to respond, and succeeded sufficiently to lift her arms and put them round his neck as he kissed her. But she was very aware of her own nakedness, of his buttons against her breasts, of the coldness of his belt-buckle, of the material of his trousers, rough against her legs.

His breathing grew heavy and he made a groaning noise deep in his throat. It was an animal-like sound, a sound that frightened her. Elaine drew back, saw the urgent hunger in his eyes, the tautness of anticipation in his face. Terror filled her. She went to speak but no sound came from her tight throat. And suddenly Calum stooped and picked her up, swung her over to the bed and put her on it.

'A moment,' he said on a thick, unsteady note. 'A moment, my darling.'

He turned away from her, giving Elaine a few precious minutes to recover a little. He had put her down on top of the bed, but she pulled back the covers and got inside it. It was, as he'd said, a big bed. Did he bring all his women here? Was that why it was so big? Her mind was in a whirl. One moment she wanted to tell him no, she didn't want this. The next she was glad it was too late for that. Tonight, one way or the other, she was going to find out many truths about herself.

She couldn't watch him undress. Pulling the covers up to her neck, she kept her head firmly turned away. She heard a drawer open and then close. The rustle of movement. And then Calum was sliding into the bed beside her.

He smiled a little when he saw the way she was clutching the sheets. 'My prim darling,' he said, his voice husky and unsteady. 'Relax, my lovely one.'

Reaching for her under the covers, he caressed her, then tried to pull down the sheet. 'The lights!' she said urgently. 'Turn off the lights.'

'But I want to look at you.'

'No! Turn them *off*!'

It was spoken in such an imperative tone that Calum lifted himself on his elbow to look at her intently for a moment, then he leaned across and flicked off the lamp.

She let go the covers, forced herself to try and relax, to let him do what he wanted.

Elaine lay on her back, staring up into the darkness, her body still as rigid as when he had tried to take her, but now her heart was frozen too. It had been dreadful. The worst experience of her life. Far worse than she could ever have imagined. Calum had been very patient with her, but turning off the light had been a terrible mistake. When he'd touched her she'd thought of Neil and her body had just seized up, flinching from his caresses, expecting to be hurt, expecting his intolerance of her fear. Calum had stroked and kissed her, whispered compliments to her that she had been too tense to hear, had whispered, 'Let me in, darling. Let me in.'

She had obeyed because the longing was still there, deep inside her, but it had been years since she'd had a

man—long before Neil had been killed—and her body
had tightened. It wouldn't have been easy that first time
anyway, but because she was so rigid, her body un-
yielding, Calum had inevitably hurt her. He had tried
not to, had tried to use his body to awaken her own
desire enough to make her relax, but in so doing had
aroused himself so much that his own need had become
urgent, undeniable, and he had thrust into her.

When she'd cried out he had gasped an apology, had
tried to take her in his arms to comfort her. 'I'm sorry,
darling. I didn't mean to hurt you. Let me hold you.'

But she had pushed him away. 'No! Leave me alone.'

'Darling, please. I——'

'Don't touch me! Leave me alone.'

He could only think that she was angry with him, and
wasn't to know how appalled she felt. So it *was* the same.
Even with someone like Calum who was so experienced.
And it must be her fault, as she'd always feared. She
was frigid, as Neil had so often accused her. She would
never know the pleasure of love that she'd read about,
would never be able to make a man happy—or herself.
For the rest of her life she would be alone, would have
to learn to stifle any sexual feelings, to make herself as
unattractive as possible to men. Because Elaine knew
that she could never go through this humiliating, degrading experience again. As kind as Calum had been,
she had never felt so ashamed, had never despised herself
so much.

She didn't cry, was past that. But every now and again
a spasm ran through her body that she was unable to
control. Calum tried to speak to her but she refused to
answer him, until presently he gave up and moved
to the other side of the bed. After a couple of hours,
when she was absolutely sure he was asleep, Elaine slid
out of bed.

Her nightdress was a pool of shimmering silver on the floor. She picked it up and pulled it on, her eyes accustomed to the darkness by now, then let herself out of the room, taking ages to turn the catch in case it clicked and woke Calum. Closing the door carefully behind her, she stood in the corridor, not really knowing what to do next. She padded soft-footed along to the sitting-room, and only then switched on a lamp. Her limbs were shaking as she poured herself a much needed drink. Not even bothering to look at what it was, she tossed it down. It was brandy; the fiery liquid hit the back of her throat, sent a degree of warmth to her numb body and a comforting shot of alcohol to her dizzy brain.

It was then, as her tension eased a little, that she began to cry. A great sob broke from her and she hastily stuffed her hand in her mouth, afraid that Calum would hear.

Opening the French windows, she went outside on to the veranda, shutting them behind her. Leaning against the wall, she stood and let the tears come, crying for what might have been and what she now knew was gone forever. They said you couldn't miss something you had never known, but that wasn't true; she knew full well that there had to be more to a relationship than what she'd just gone through, and she wept not for its loss but for the fact that she would never know it. Other women, such fortunate women, would have loving relationships, would have children, but those were not for her; she was alone and always would be.

Her sadness engulfed her, but through it she became aware of a rumbling noise in the distance, like the noise of a plane high in the sky. It stopped for a few moments then came again, louder this time. Dragging her head up, she looked in the direction of the noise. As she watched, a flash of lightning lit the distant sky behind the hills, followed by a clap of thunder. It came nearer,

the thunderclaps louder. She felt no fear; she had always
been fascinated by storms. Her eyes still on the sky, she
went down the steps and into the garden, just as she
was, to watch.

The brandy had warmed her through so that she didn't
feel at all cold. Standing on the lawn, she was able to
see the approaching storm more clearly. Instead of just
the flash, she saw the lightning itself—great jagged arms
of crackling light which seemed to touch the hills and
set them on fire. The thunder now was very loud—great
claps which hurt her ears. Quite unafraid of its nearness,
she felt thrilled by it, enraptured, all her own problems
lost beneath the awesome hand of nature. She had seen
electric storms before, of course, but never one of such
fierce energy, never one that rampaged across the
countryside, tearing the sky apart, turning night into day.

The next thunderclap was even closer, seemed almost
in the next valley. With it came rain, great drops that
pelted like pennies tossed from the sky, hard, but
strangely not cold. Elaine turned her head up to them,
felt them wet on her lips, all mixed up with her tears.
She opened her mouth to drink them in, stood in an
attitude of suppliance to the gods of the storm. Lightning
worked down from the sky, lit every building in the
quinta, seemed to run along the ground among the vines.
Somewhere an animal cried in terror, but the sound was
drowned by the storm, just as Calum shouting her name
was lost in the next thunderclap.

She didn't know he was there until he ran up to her
and caught her arm. 'Elaine! Come inside.' He had
hastily pulled on a pair of sleeping-shorts, but wore
nothing else.

'No. Listen to it. Look at it.' Her eyes wide and excited, she shook him off.

Calum stared at her, amazed by what he saw. 'The lightning—it's dangerous,' he shouted.

Elaine laughed and ran a few steps away from him. 'No, it's fantastic.' She whirled round, the soaking nightgown clinging to her body, revealing every curve. 'Go in if you're afraid.'

'Elaine, this is crazy.' Calum came after her, pushing his wet hair out of his eyes. 'Come inside. We could be killed.'

'So, what the hell?' The lightning seemed to have filled her full of fire. She felt overflowing with brittle energy, intoxicated with excitement. She danced round again and laughed as Calum reached for her and she eluded him.

The sky seemed to erupt into light and sound as the lightning broke immediately above them. Elaine stood still to stare and Calum caught her. He would have picked her up and carried her inside, but his fingers slipped on the wet silk and she turned within his hold, tried to push him away. They struggled together, the rain plastering their hair to their heads, getting in their eyes. Legs and bodies rubbed and strained against each other as they both tried to exert their will. But then, quite suddenly, Elaine wasn't struggling any more. Her arms went round him and she was kissing him fiercely, clinging to him, her body crushed against his.

Calum lifted his head with a cry of amazement, unable to believe the change in her. With a peal of laughter she broke from him again and ran among the trees, dodging behind them as he came after her.

'You idiot! Get away from the trees.'

She went to slip away from him again but he anticipated her action and caught her, swung her up into his arms before she could get away. Another great crash of lightning came as he ran with her into the open. Behind them a small tree was hit and burst into flame, only to be put out immediately in hissing anger by the rain. Calum would have carried her inside but Elaine put her arms round his neck and kissed him again with a hunger that was as savage as the storm.

Suddenly, his foot slipped on the wet grass and he went down on his knees. Elaine still clung to him, her kisses devouring him, sending everything else out of his mind. Suddenly he was tearing at her nightdress, dragging it from her, pulling off his own shorts, and then they were on the ground, almost fighting each other again in their eagerness to kiss and touch and hold.

The lawn sloped and they rolled together, their legs entwined, Elaine's hands on either side of his head, drinking in his mouth, taking the rain from his lips with her tongue. They came to a stop with her underneath him. She felt his arousal and gripped his shoulders as she arched towards him, her body a slender bow, her breath a gasping plea of panting eagerness. Calum gave a groan of agonised excitement, and put his arm underneath her to lift her towards him, taking her now willing, hungry body as another great clap of thunder filled the night.

But even that great noise wasn't enough to drown out his cry of frenzied rapture, or Elaine's rising moans as, for the first time, she discovered that love could be more than just a duty, could transcend every other emotion she'd ever known. Her excitement peaked into a great crescendo of ecstasy, was held there for the most wonderful moment of her life. Slowly it faded, leaving her whole and new, and with tears on her face again, but of happiness and gratitude now. Then she lay back on the grass, her heart beating crazily, Calum's arm across her, and listened as the storm gradually faded into the distance.

Picking her up, Calum carried her into the house and stood her under the shower, joining her there as the hot water ran over them. He soaped the grass from her, let his fingers run through her hair as the water rinsed it clean. Often he stopped to kiss her, holding her against him, and she returned his kisses with warmth and eagerness, the enchantment of their lovemaking still in her eyes.

He dried her off, using a towel warm from the airing-cupboard, then took out another and would have dried himself, but she took the towel from his hands and, with a great light of new awareness in her eyes, rubbed it over him. She was able to look at him now, able to marvel at the beauty of his body and, knowing it was safe, to touch him lightly.

'You witch,' Calum breathed.

He kissed her but then she pulled away from him. 'I'd like some talc on, please.'

'Would you, indeed? There should be some of Francesca's here.' He found both the talc and a huge powder-puff and dabbed it on her, greatly enjoying himself.

When every inch of her had been covered she took the puff from him. 'Now it's your turn.'

'You don't seriously want me to go around smelling of that feminine stuff, do you? I shall get strange looks. Here.' He found some of his own. 'Use this.'

It was in a container that you shook over yourself, so she smoothed it over him with her hands. She started at his shoulders and worked down, but didn't get very far. Just far enough to know that he wanted her, yet again.

And this time, when he carried her to the bed, it was slow and right and wonderful. It was lovemaking and not sex; it was sharing and not being used. Importantly, it confirmed the fact that she was a beautiful, desirable

woman. It taught her again the joy of excited rapture
that a woman could experience, and most of all it taught
her that it was possible to place her trust in a man. With
a sigh of contentment, Elaine knew that she had come
alive at last.

CHAPTER SIX

THEY both slept late, but it was Elaine who woke first, woke to think for a minute that she'd been having the most fantastic dream, and the next moment realising it was true. There could be no better awakening than that. She knew it and treasured the feeling.

The sun was already high, seeping through the unshuttered windows and the lace curtains. Beside her Calum lay asleep on his back, his profile turned towards her. Inching up in the bed until she was sitting, Elaine looked down at him, studying him, seeing him now as her lover and not just as a man. Lover. What an evocative word it was. Elaine savoured it, letting it roll round her mind. Once it had meant that a man loved you, wrote poems to you, might have no hope of winning you but was your devoted admirer. Now, of course, it meant that you had gone to bed with a man and that the relationship might, or might not, be an ongoing one. But it meant a whole lot more than a one-night stand, definitely more than that.

Calum looked so very handsome even in sleep, his skin tanned to that golden-bronze colour, just enough, not too deep as some men liked and which would eventually turn their skin to leather. The sheet was down almost to his waist, and she could see that his skin was soft and his chest smooth where it gently rose as he breathed. His lashes were slightly darker than his hair and long, brushing his cheeks as he slept. His face, with his fair hair, ought to have looked feminine, but it was entirely masculine, perhaps because of the leanness of his fea-

tures, the clear-cut line of his jaw and the thinness of
his mouth.

Looking at him, Elaine felt almost as if she was seeing
him for the first time, because now she was looking at
him as a part of her life and not just an interesting man.
Now she would take what she saw into her heart and
remember him forever.

She felt an intense gratitude towards him for giving
her this priceless gift. But it could all have gone so
frightfully wrong, would have done if it hadn't been for
the storm, so perhaps she should thank divine provi-
dence instead. There again, she now remembered that
she'd had an extremely large brandy, so perhaps she
should thank the god Bacchus, too.

'You look like the Mona Lisa,' Calum commented,
awake and watching her. 'She has that kind of smile on
her face.'

Elaine's smile deepened. 'For the same reason, do you
think?'

'You're a woman—you should know.'

Her eyes widened a little as she realised that she was
indeed now fully a woman. 'So I am,' she said softly.

Calum lifted a hand and let his finger travel up the
length of her bare arm. 'Of course, the Mona Lisa had
some clothes on.' She gave a soft sigh, her lips parting
at the deliciousness of his touch. 'You look like a
gorgeous tortoiseshell cat, with the sunlight coming
through the curtains on to you, and with your hair—
your beautiful hair—like molten copper down your
back.'

His finger reached her shoulder, traced the column of
her throat, her chin, then started the journey slowly down
her breast, hovered at the nipple, gently, exquisitely caressing it into springing awareness before carrying on
down to her waist.

'Are you all right?' he asked softly.

It was natural that he should ask; it had been so bad that first time and he knew he'd hurt her. But his question wasn't only to ask how she was physically; she knew that he was also asking how she felt emotionally.

Her eyes warm, smiling, she said, 'I'm fine. Really fine.' And she bent to kiss him, her hair falling forward, cutting out the light, creating a small private world for them both.

Calum took hold of her shoulders and, when she went to lift herself up, wouldn't let her, instead holding her head against his so that the kiss deepened, became hot and urgent. Against her mouth he said, 'There is really only one way to make love in the morning.' And, pulling her down on to him, he showed her how, showed her until his tawny cat threw back her head to cry out her long, agonising pleasure, then collapsed purring against his chest.

'What would you like to do today?' Calum asked her languidly some time later, when their hearts had stopped hammering and she was lying contentedly in his arms.

'Don't you have to get back to Oporto? To go to work?'

'Are you kidding?'

The indignant amazement in his voice made her smile happily, pleased that he wanted her enough to stay on. 'Can we go on your boat?'

'Of course. A wonderful idea.' He glanced at the clock, saw how late it was. 'We won't bother with a picnic; we'll moor near some small town or village and walk up to the nearest café.' Then he sat up and clicked his fingers. 'Better still, why don't we take a few clothes with us and spend the night on the boat? That way I'll be able to show you far more of the river.'

'That sounds great.' Elaine didn't ask him again if he could spare the time; she was just glad that he didn't want to leave her.

They hurried to get ready, Elaine going to her own room to shower and dress. She felt supremely happy and, glancing at herself in the mirror as she towelled herself dry, could hardly believe she was the same person she had been yesterday. That poor, nervous, fearful creature was gone forever. Now she was whole, and ready to enjoy life. And boy, was she going to make the most of it!

The earth smelt sweet and fresh after the storm, seemed already greener, and there were wild flowers everywhere.

'Do you have many storms like last night's?' Elaine asked as they walked down to the boat.

'Electric storms? Yes, they happen all the time.' Calum smiled. 'But I've never known one quite like last night's.'

'Really?' She raised her eyebrows.

'I'll never forget it,' he answered, his eyes holding hers. 'It was special—and so are you.'

She glowed with pleasure, her face alive with it.

'You seem so different today,' Calum said wonderingly.

One of her brilliant smiles lit her face. 'Of course. I *am* different.'

A movement on the river caught her eye. It was the cruise boat, going back the other way, the one she'd seen when she'd been alone a few days ago. It seemed impossible that her life could have changed so much in such a short time; then she'd been wondering if Calum would even bother to come to the *quinta*; now they were lovers. She waved to the boat, then looked round at Calum and found him watching her with a strangely pensive expression.

'What is it?'

He blinked, as if coming back to earth, but then shook his head. 'Let's get the boat out on to the river. You'll have to crew for me today.'

There wasn't really much to do once they were on the river, but when they moored for lunch Elaine had to jump on to the bank with the rope so that they could secure the boat. Several children appeared from nowhere to help and were enlisted by Calum to guard the boat while they walked up into the village. They ate a simple meal of freshly baked bread and cheese made from goat's milk, which Calum called 'cheese of the mountains', with a crisp salad and a bottle of *vinho verde*.

On the way back Calum bought her a straw hat from a cave of a shop hung with baskets and woven mats. It was the type of hat the workers wore out in the vine fields, to keep off the winter rain and the summer sun.

'I don't want you getting sunstroke,' he told her.

Elaine put it on, jamming it over her hair, which was loose and still wildly curly from the shower. 'How does that look?' Putting her hands on her hips, she struck a coquettish pose.

Calum laughed, but then his eyes darkened a little as they went over her, and he put his arm round her waist. 'Seductive.'

They were both wearing shorts and his leg was against hers—deliberately. It was a warm, intimate moment, acknowledging that they were close, promising that they would be again.

There was a little market in the village, noisy and full of life. They bought some food and wine and went back to the boat. The little boys were still standing guard and were all solemnly rewarded, making them break out into huge smiles and rush off into the village to spend their wages.

They went on upriver, Calum at the wheel, with Elaine beside him on the double seat as he steered, sometimes letting her take over when there was a straight stretch with no other craft. That was easy and fun, but she preferred to look out at the passing scenery, at old arched stone bridges over bubbling tributaries, carrying roads or the railway line. Sometimes, among the trees, there would be a large new house, often in the baroque style, the red pantiles of the roof and white-painted walls standing out against the green of the hills, waiting for the sun to weather them until they dissolved into the landscape.

Gradually the terrain changed until the river was running through a deep, narrow gorge.

'There used to be very strong rapids here before the dam was built,' Calum told her. 'One of my ancestors was drowned when his boat hit a rock.'

'When was that?'

'Around 1850.'

'Was he alone?'

'No, there were several ladies in the party but they were saved because their crinolines held them up until they could be rescued. Unfortunately, my ancestor, yet another Calum Lennox Brodey, was wearing a belt full of gold sovereigns to pay his farmers with, and it carried him down. His body was never found.'

'What a terrible thing to happen.'

Calum nodded. 'He was quite an important man in the region. All the flags in Oporto flew at half-mast when they heard the news.'

As they would if anything happened to Calum or his grandfather, Elaine realised. For a while she had forgotten his position, his wealth, forgotten that up until a few days ago he had virtually been her employer, certainly a valued client. Last night, and definitely tonight,

they would be just a man and a woman, as close as any
had been since time began, but she must remember that
it was to be just a brief affair, could never be more than
that. However much she was involved with Calum
physically, she mustn't let her emotions grow beyond
friendship and a deep gratitude.

When the sun began to go down they moored the boat
away from any town, out near the open fields where no
one would go by. They ate their supper, drank the wine,
unhurriedly, but knowing that they were going to make
love. Through the windows they watched the sun set,
red and gold, a miracle of colours. Then they drew the
curtains to shut out the world.

This time Calum did as he'd wanted the night before,
slowly undressing her, then letting her do the same to
him, something she had never done before. They sat
together on the edge of the bed in the cabin, kissing,
stroking, each looking with awed delight at the beauty
of the other. Then Calum laid her down and kissed her
full length before leaning over her.

For a moment he gazed down at her, at her parted
lips and eyes full of desire, at the glow of anticipation
on her hot skin, at her body which was eager for him
to take her. His voice thick and unsteady, he said, 'You
were made for love, Elaine. Made for this.' And then he
came down on to her, carrying her with him as they both
reached the peak of sexual pleasure, their excitement
equally intense as their bodies became one, the climax
long and exquisite for them both.

They made love twice more during the night, Calum
once kissing her awake, his body avid for her yet again,
lifting her from sleep into swift, hungry passion.

Waves from a passing vessel gently rocked the boat
the next morning, wakening them. They were already
close in each other's arms, this bed being much smaller

than the one in Calum's room back at the *quinta*. Calum stretched the arm she'd been lying on and smiled at her. 'Good morning, my lovely one.'

'Did I hurt your arm?' Elaine asked, propping herself on her elbow.

'No, you fitted perfectly.' Putting his hand behind her head, he drew her down to kiss her. Then he raised an eyebrow. 'Well?'

'Well what?'

'What are you waiting for?' She looked puzzled, so he said, 'Didn't I show you yesterday the only way to wake up in the morning?'

Elaine smiled, and moved over him.

The shower in the boat was so small that there was only room for one of them at a time, but Calum kept putting his hand round the curtain until she splashed some water at him, then they made a game of it, the boat carpet getting very wet in the process. Laughing, pretending to be afraid of her, Calum pulled on a pair of shorts, went on deck and dived into the river for a swim. As she dried herself and dressed in shorts and a low sun-top, Elaine found herself grinning like an idiot, she was so happy. Calum climbed back on board and showered and dressed while she made breakfast, which they carried out to the cockpit and ate on the long seat there, basking in the morning sun.

Afterwards, Calum leaned back and ran a finger down her spine. 'I feel extremely lazy,' he murmured.

'I'm surprised you have any strength left at all,' she remarked, with awe for his virility in her voice.

'Do you want to tell me about it, my sweet?'

She knew what he meant but was disconcerted by the question, especially coming now, when that first dreadful time had been almost forgotten, buried under the wonderful times they had been close since. She sat forward so that he couldn't see her face. 'It?' she said to gain time.

'You know what I mean; there was far more to cause you to be so tense the first time we made love than just nervousness.'

'I was bound to feel nervous.'

'Yes. And I expected it. But there *was* more to it than that, wasn't there?'

For a long moment she was silent, wishing that he hadn't asked her, wishing that she hadn't been reminded of her past, not when she was so happy. Turning to look at him, her eyes troubled, she said, 'Yes, of course there was. I'm sorry about it. I know it was my fault. I know it spoilt that first time for you terribly.'

Watching her closely, Calum said, 'You turned away from me afterwards, wouldn't let me touch you, acted as if I was some kind of monster.'

'I'm sorry,' she said wretchedly.

'I don't want you to apologise, darling. I want you to tell me why. Nothing like that has ever happened to me before. I was so afraid I'd hurt you, and horrified by your reaction. When the storm woke me and I found you gone, I was so afraid that you—that you'd been driven to do something stupid.'

Her eyes widened as Elaine stared at him in appalled dismay. 'Oh, Calum, I had no idea. I didn't realise.'

He gave a rather grim smile. 'It was quite a relief to find you out in the garden. But even then you were in danger from the lightning.' His eyes softened as he remembered. 'Crazy idiot, dancing around out there in the middle of an electric storm.'

'Did you think I'd flipped?'

'Until you kissed me and I realised you'd been drinking.'

'I did have a rather large brandy,' Elaine admitted.

'So I gathered.'

She gave him an admonishing look. 'Are you telling me that you'd take advantage of a drunken woman?'

'If it made her respond the way you did, then yes, any time,' Calum responded promptly.

Elaine laughed and gave him a playful punch, but then, serious again, said, 'Maybe I was a little intoxicated, but it was the storm that put me on a high. It was so close, so primeval—the most fantastic storm I'd ever seen. Nature erupting all around us.'

'Remind me never to take you near a volcano,' Calum said drily.

He looked at her, waiting for her to answer his original question. Elaine bit her lip, then shook her head. 'I'm sorry, but I don't want to talk about it. Not now. Not here. These two days have been so wonderful; don't let's spoil them.'

'Would it spoil them, then?'

'Oh, yes, I'm sure of it.'

He hesitated, then gave her a quizzical look. 'Don't you trust me enough, Elaine?'

The question surprised her. 'It has nothing to do with trust.' She grew a little annoyed that he wouldn't let the subject go. 'It has nothing to do with you. I want to forget all that, not talk about it.'

'I'm sorry,' Calum said stiffly.

She realised that tension was starting to build between them and hastily sought to dispel it. 'Shall we sail on? Where shall we go to?' Standing up as she spoke, she collected up the breakfast things and took them into the galley.

Calum watched her, saying nothing more, but there was a frown between his brows and the question was still in his eyes.

They sailed on to the next town where they had lunch, but in the afternoon moored in a tributary that came straight down from the hills and swam in a large pool formed by its waters. It was cold, making Elaine gasp, but such fun to play around with Calum in the water. He was a really good swimmer, often diving down and coming up first behind her, his arms taking her by surprise as they encircled her, or else surging out of the water, lifting her with him and kissing her at the same time.

Back on the boat they made love again, the curtains open because no one there could possibly see them, the sun pouring through the windows on to their panting, thrusting bodies.

That evening they sailed back to the *quinta*, where they found that the house had been cleaned and the fridge replenished by Senhora Varosa. Elaine began to prepare a meal while Calum phoned his office. It was some time before he joined her, carrying two glasses of white port. Elaine took one from him but, looking at his face, knew that it was over.

'You have to go back to Oporto,' she said flatly.

'I'm afraid so. There's a business meeting I have to attend early tomorrow morning. I tried to get out of it, or delay it, but there's just no way round it. I wish there were. I would have given a great deal to stay on with you here.' He lifted his glass in a toast. 'To you, my darling Elaine. To thank you for these two very wonderful days.'

'When will you have to leave?'

'Later tonight. I'll take one of the *quinta* cars and leave mine here for you to use for the rest of your holiday.'

'Can you come back?'

'Not till the weekend. How much longer can you stay?'

'I have to be in England for a fashion show on Saturday. I'm doing the catering for it.'

'Can't you delegate it?'

Elaine shook her head unhappily. 'We're doing a wedding as well that day; I have to be there. I really ought to go back earlier.'

'Don't.' Calum came to a decision. 'Look, somehow I'll rearrange my schedule so that I can come here again on Friday morning. We'll have the day together——' he smiled warmly '—and the night, then I'll take you into Oporto early on Saturday morning to catch a plane. Will that be OK with you?'

She had anticipated going home at least a day earlier but, like him, Elaine was unable to resist the thought of some more time together. So she nodded eagerly. 'Oh, yes.'

'Wonderful!' Calum hugged her, then looked down at her, letting desire come into his eyes as he held her. 'And we do, of course, have tonight.'

So this time they didn't linger over their meal, were soon in bed, making love with the heightened passion and awareness of two people who knew they were soon to be parted. For them it would only be for a couple of days, but even so there was a kind of frenzy tonight that hadn't been there before. It made them more than ever eager to give pleasure to the other, to make it memorable, to lift them both to a new plane of sensual excitement.

Calum stayed with her till the last minute, then had to drag himself away to dress, only just ready when a car horn hooted outside as one of the *quinta* workers brought it round.

'I won't bother to pack. Here are the keys to my car; you're quite sure you feel confident enough to drive it?'

'Yes, of course.' Still sitting in the bed, the sheet down to her waist on her naked body, she held out her arms to say goodbye to him.

Calum gave a groan and came to kneel beside her and take her in his arms. They had been naked together so much that it seemed strange now to feel his clothes against her skin. He bent to kiss her breasts, his lips now familiar, but still capable of immediately arousing her. 'God, it's so hard to leave you. These two days have meant so much to me, my beautiful Elaine.' He hesitated, then smiled. 'Don't leave this bed till I get back.'

She laughed and put her hands on either side of his face to look deep into his eyes. 'Thank you, Calum.'

There was such intensity in her voice that Calum immediately sensed it was for something far more than their time together. 'Tell me just one thing,' he said, his voice suddenly urgent. 'Why me? Why did you choose me to be the first one since your husband died?'

Elaine hesitated a fraction too long before saying on a flippant note, 'You may not have noticed, but you're not at all bad-looking, Brodey.'

He shook off the compliment. 'There are millions like me in the world. So why me?'

She gave a small, uneasy laugh. 'I fancied you, of course.'

Putting his hands on her shoulders, Calum looked intently into her eyes. 'Fancied me? Was that all?'

Elaine had been brought up always to be truthful and so found it difficult to lie. Not that she wanted to lie to him, because he'd been so wonderful to her, but she tried now, saying, 'What else would there be? And why all these questions? I thought you were in a hurry.'

But he saw through her quite easily, and said insistently, 'Why else, Elaine? Tell me.'

She gave an uneasy sigh and said reluctantly, 'I felt
that the time was right, that I needed to find out if I
could...' Her voice trailed away.

He didn't seem to mind that; he nodded. 'That's
understandable. So when we met...?'

Elaine nodded eagerly, glad that it was OK. 'When I
saw you I liked you, and I knew it would be sa——' She
stopped precipitately, wishing she could bite off her
tongue, tried to cover it by adding in a rush, 'I knew
that you were experienced and that——'

But Calum picked up on her fluster at once, as she'd
known he would. 'No,' he interrupted. 'That wasn't what
you were going to say. What was it?' His grip tightened
a little. 'Tell me.'

She stared up into his eyes, then gave a small shrug.
'All right. I knew that this would happen.'

He frowned, not expecting this answer. 'This? What
do you mean?'

'That we'd part. That you'd go back to Oporto and
I'd go home. That we would never see one another
again.' She felt his body stiffen, but added truthfully, 'I
knew that an affair with you would be safe. There would
be no—complications afterwards.'

Letting go of her shoulders, Calum drew back, his
face hardening as he stared at her for long seconds. 'Do
you know how much of an insult that is?' he demanded
harshly.

'I'm sorry; I didn't want to——'

But he had got to his feet and stood looking down at
her with a fierce anger in his eyes. 'So you decided to
use me.' His voice full of bitterness, he said, 'Tell me,
Elaine—just what difference is there between you and a
bitch like Tiffany Dean?' Then he turned and strode out
of the room.

*   *   *

So she'd blown it. So what? It had been about to end anyway. On Saturday Calum would have taken her to the airport, they would have said goodbye, and that would have been it. What difference would spending one more day together have made, for heaven's sake?

Elaine went on at herself like this for hours—after her stunned mind had accepted the fact that everything had changed so quickly. For a long time she had just sat and stared at the door, unable to believe that he had gone, had walked out on her without another word. It had all happened so rapidly, within minutes. One moment he was saying a loving goodbye to her, the next he was dragging that silly little confession out of her, and his warmth and tenderness had changed to something close to hate.

It seemed unbelievable that it had happened, that her wonderful affair had ended so badly. For there could be no doubt that it had ended; Calum would never come back as they'd arranged. And there was no way she wanted to stay on here alone. It would be pointless without the hope of seeing him again. And besides, this was Calum's house; how could she possibly stay here when she had offended him so much?

Feeling deeply dejected, Elaine lay back on her pillow, her hand resting where he had so recently been lying, and tried to see it from Calum's point of view, to understand why he'd been so angry. She couldn't see it. Men were supposed to be flattered if a woman fancied them, made a play for them. They were also supposed to take advantage of it and not want the affair to get serious. Really, she had played by the rules. So why had he got so angry? Had she really used him? Perhaps. But he hadn't been coerced in any way; he needn't have come up to the *quinta*. And it was he who had sent Francesca away so that they'd be alone here, she remembered indignantly.

From feeling wretched about it, Elaine began to feel angry herself. There had been no need for him to be so rude to her. It hadn't needed to end like that. A thought occurred to her: had he provoked that argument deliberately? Had he been afraid that she might be getting serious and wanted to make a clean break of it? After all, he hadn't known that she wanted to end it too.

But that couldn't be right. It had been Calum who had pressed her to stay on, to be here when he could get back; he'd pressed her eagerly. And why should he think she might be getting serious? She hadn't said she loved him or anything. She'd been careful not to, even when they'd been making love. Admittedly she'd told him he was wonderful a few times—perhaps rather more than a few, she realised fairly, but that was nothing compared to the endearments and compliments he had showered on her.

Would she have been so insulted if it had been the other way round? The thought stole into her mind. What if she'd found out that Calum had only wanted her because he'd known that it would be a short casual affair without any strings? But she'd taken that for granted, had expected it all along. OK, maybe her pride would be hurt a little, but surely it wouldn't have made her so angry that she'd walk out on him? She would only feel like that if she cared about him, only if she really cared. But Calum couldn't possibly care for her like that, so maybe it *was* just his pride that had been hurt. After all, the Brodeys were an extremely proud family, especially Calum; one only had to look at the way he'd turned on Tiffany when he'd found out she was a cheat.

From anger she went back to feeling desolate again. Those two days had been so wonderful; she ought to have known it was too good to be true. A great sense of loss filled her when she realised that she would never see Calum again. But she had expected that, had known it would happen. The thought didn't help, however. She knew that she would be lonely without him, would ache for a long time to have him in her arms again, yearn for him to be with her, loving her.

Reaching out, she stroked the pillow where his head had rested, remembered the first time they had been in this bed, and how kind he had been to her. She cried then a little, until she remembered how gloriously everything had changed. Calum had given her back her womanhood, her love of life. Nothing could take that from her, not now. She would cherish it and remember him always, gratefully, lovingly.

Falling asleep at last, Elaine woke early the next morning feeling sad but very philosophical. She had breakfast, packed, and put her cases in the car. Then she took a last walk down to the river, memorising every detail of the scenery, so that she could look back on it whenever she needed to. She walked back slowly, her feet disturbing the wild flowers, filling the air with their scent. There was still a scrap of white silk on the lawn, the remains of the nightdress Calum had torn from her that night of the storm. Elaine picked it up, twisted it between her fingers, smiling.

From the garden she went into the house, walking through the rooms, saying goodbye to it, touching the furniture, the bed, all the time remembering. Only then did she walk down through the *quinta* to Senhora Varosa's house, to tell her that she was leaving. The housekeeper and all her family came to see her off, the children waving and running beside the car until she turned out of the gate.

Luckily she had left nothing at the *palácio* so she drove
straight to the airport. There she was just in time to get
a seat on a charter flight leaving for London within a
couple of hours. Buying an envelope and a stamp, she
put the car keys inside and addressed it to Calum at the
palácio. She dropped it into the mail-box without en-
closing a letter or even a note. It was better this way.
Her holiday affair was over and it was time to go home.

CHAPTER SEVEN

THE fashion show was a great success. Elaine, her part
in the organisation over, was able to stand in the background and watch as the matchstick-thin models paraded
along the catwalk, displaying clothes that took her breath
away. Some of them, of course, were quite outrageous,
but there were several outfits that she really liked. Before
her trip to Portugal, before those days of love with
Calum, she would have just looked and done nothing;
now it occurred to her that she might look good in them
herself. Not giving herself time to have second thoughts,
Elaine made appointments with a couple of the designer
houses there and then.

That evening, when she got home, she went immediately through the post, then hurried to listen to the messages on the answering machine. There was nothing from
Calum. There had been no word from him since she'd
got back to England. She tried hard not to feel disappointed, telling herself that she hadn't really expected to
hear from him. Although she still didn't understand why
he had been so very angry; it seemed strangely out of
proportion to the offence. Maybe his masculine pride
had been hurt; combined with Brodey arrogance, that
added up to something pretty awesome. She sighed,
wishing that she could have kept him as a friend at least.

Going into her bedroom, Elaine went through her
wardrobe and decided that she hated every single thing
she owned. The suits she'd worn for business, although
smart, were all in dark colours. So too were the evening
clothes, her 'dissolving into the background' outfits. But

why the hell should she have to lose herself in the wall-paper? She was the head of a successful, up-market business and she had as much right to dress as fashionably and colourfully as anyone else. For heaven's sake, she wasn't even thirty and yet she looked like a dowd. Her whole image, she decided, was wrong, and had to be changed at once. She would go on a diet, take more exercise and have something done to her hair. And first thing Monday she would go shopping for some new clothes.

The next day there was a christening party that she had to supervise, but on the following morning she rang the office to say that she would be late and went on her shopping spree. It was one of the best days she'd had; she enjoyed herself so much that it was mid-afternoon before she finally arrived at her office, so loaded with parcels that the taxi-driver had to help carry them for her.

'Good heavens! What happened to you?' Ruth, her secretary, exclaimed as she came forward to help.

'I got a bit carried away,' Elaine admitted as she paid the driver and thanked him. 'I hope you haven't been too busy?'

'Nothing I couldn't handle, although there are several people that you'll have to phone back. Oh, and those flowers arrived for you.' She nodded towards Elaine's own desk.

'From the fashion-show people, I expect,' Elaine said, going across. 'What a beautiful arrangement. They have been generous.'

She moved the basket of flowers on to a shelf by the window and sat down to read through her messages and make the answering calls. It kept her busy for nearly an hour, making several appointments to go and visit people to discuss their requirements—something she always insisted on, to make sure that she knew exactly what people wanted and could see where a function was to be held.

Once, early on, she had accepted a customer's word that there was plenty of room in her house for a reception for a hundred people, but to her horror Elaine had found, when they went to set everything up, that it was far too small. By then, of course, it had been quite impossible to hire a marquee. Luckily, it had been a beautiful day and she had put all the children outside at a makeshift table, but it had taught her always to go and see for herself.

Sitting at the phone as she waited for one customer to get her guest-list, Elaine's eyes were drawn to the flowers. The fashion-show organisers had really been very generous: there were lilies in the arrangement and the most beautiful orchids, their scent filling the air. The accompanying card, in the usual sealed florist's envelope, was just visible among the blooms near the basket's rim.

Suddenly Elaine dropped the phone and strode over to take out the card. Her fingers fumbling maddeningly, she took it out. Her heart jumped when she saw the words 'Calum Brodey', but the message was quite short. 'With grateful thanks for all the hard work which made our bicentennial so successful.'

Elaine stared down at the card, not knowing what to make of it. It was so cold, so formal. As if he were just a customer, had never been anything more. He must, then, still be angry with her. Yet he had sent the flowers, and they were so beautiful. She bent to smell them, closed her eyes and could see again the garden at the *quinta*, the walk down to the boat with honeysuckle trailing from the trees . . .

A squawking sound from the desk made her remember her phone call and she ran back to it, and was kept busy for the next quarter of an hour. But she put the card down on her desk and her troubled eyes went back to it often.

Ned and Malcolm called in to give her a progress report on some advance work they'd been doing for a big wedding in Gloucestershire at the weekend.

'You know, I think it would almost be worth our while to buy our own marquee; we seem to use one so often,' Malcolm remarked.

'Perhaps, but then we'd have to store it somewhere and hire men to put it up every time. And they cost so much that I'm not sure we could justify the outlay. But I'll look into it and try and work out some figures,' she promised, always pleased when one of her employees came up with an idea.

They left soon afterwards, offering Ruth a lift home, so that Elaine was left alone. There were more calls that she should have made, but as soon as they'd gone she picked up the card from Calum and read it again. Not that she needed to: she knew its brief message by heart now. The writing, she realised, wasn't Calum's, but then it wouldn't be; it had probably been written by someone at the florist's after getting the instructions from Portugal.

She frowned, wondering just what Calum had meant. Was she to take his cold message, his avoidance of any endearment, as a further intimation that he wanted nothing more to do with her? Or were the flowers his way of saying that he was sorry that it had ended the way it did, a kind of proud apology?

Ordinarily when Elaine received this kind of gift, which she quite often did, she would immediately phone or send a note of thanks to the donor. Now she didn't know what to do. Was Calum expecting her to call him, or would he resent even hearing her voice? She thumped the desk in sudden anger. Damn the man! How dared he put her in this kind of quandary?

Deciding to shelve the question, she put on her jacket and went to leave—but when she got to the door she looked back, then went and picked up the flowers and took them home with her.

During the next week Elaine kept to her determined effort to change her lifestyle. She booked into a health club for an hour's session every morning, started to diet, and went to a really good hairdresser. Her hair had a natural curl that during the last ten years she had tried to keep under control, but now she remembered the way that Calum had loved to twine it round his fingers. Taking a deep breath, she told the stylist to let it have its way.

When it was done Elaine looked apprehensively in the mirror, then gave a small gasp of pleasure. Parted in the middle, her hair hung loose and full, making her look so much younger and with-it. That, and her new clothes, made her feel like a new person. But then, she was a new person, thanks to Calum.

She had still done nothing about the flowers. But the following Sunday she wrote him a short note thanking him for them, and added, after much soul-searching, 'I will always remember my stay in Portugal. Yours, Elaine.' Calum had sent the flowers to her office so she sent the letter to his, but marked the envelope 'Personal'. A secretary or someone might still open it, but at least they wouldn't learn anything from it. Not that Calum would either, she realised, but perhaps he would take that word 'personal' as it was meant. Without giving herself time to change her mind, she took the letter to the nearest pillar-box, then went jogging round the park.

It was all very well having a new image and new clothes, Elaine found, but it was more difficult to start to develop a new social life when you'd been married to a possessive husband for over six years and had deliberately cut yourself off in order to build up a business for the next three.

But it was only a week or so later that she met a man, Hugh Steventon, at a big society wedding that her company had arranged. She was wearing one of her new outfits—a burnt-orange suit in an unusual style—and he mistook her for one of the guests, so she played along for a little while before enlightening him. He was surprised at first, saying, 'You don't look like a high-powered businesswoman.'

'Why not?' Elaine came right out and asked.

'If I answered that truthfully you'd think I was flattering you,' he answered.

She liked the subtle way of complimenting her, took it as a fillip to her new image. But she said, 'Don't you approve of businesswomen, then?'

'On the contrary, I'm full of admiration. I'm all for women being independent,' he told her. 'My sister runs her own horse-breeding business.'

'Is she successful?'

'Very. Two of the horses she bred have been entered for the Derby this year.'

'And you?' she asked.

'I'm an art historian. I work as an adviser for one of the big four.'

'"The big four"?'

'Sorry. They're the four major auction houses. I arrange sales and travel around looking at pictures, that kind of thing.'

'What a delightful way to live.' Her face lit up, her imagination excited.

They talked some more until she had to excuse herself to make sure that everything was running smoothly, that the fork-supper was ready to be served and that the wedding-cake had been cut into enough pieces. The bride and groom left for their honeymoon amid a positive cascade of confetti, the car hung with 'JUST MARRIED' placards and trailing tin cans. The guests started to take their leave and Elaine and her staff to pack everything away.

Elaine was supervising the loading of the van in a courtyard at the back of the house when Hugh came looking for her.

'I've tracked you down at last,' he said with a smile. Putting his hand under her elbow, he drew her to one side. 'Come for a walk round the garden with me for a few minutes.'

'I'm really terribly busy.'

'Just five minutes. I want to ask you something.'

'All right. Take over, will you, please, Malcolm?' She handed over the clipboard with the list she was marking off. 'I've counted four baskets of linen so far.'

'You're very efficient,' Hugh remarked as they walked through an archway and into the formal gardens.

'I try to be.' She gave him a closer glance. He was older than herself, she thought, but not by much. Probably a bit younger than Calum. And he was shorter than him, too, with much darker hair. Also, where Hugh's looks could be called quite attractive, they became commonplace when compared with Calum's striking handsomeness. Elaine pulled herself up sharply, realising what she was doing. 'What did you want to ask me?' she said quickly.

'Two things. First, I'd like you to organise a surprise party for my parents' fortieth wedding anniversary in a couple of months' time.'

'Of course; I'd be happy to give you a quote for it.'

He smiled at that. 'I hardly think that will be necessary.'

'I'd rather. Really.'

'All right.'

'And the second thing?'

'I'm taking a small group of people to the races next week. I wondered if you'd care to come. Then you could meet my sister and have a talk about the party,' he added smoothly when he saw her hesitate.

Elaine smiled inwardly, realising he was coercing her a little, but not altogether displeased. 'What day next week?'

'What day are you free?' he countered.

That made her laugh openly. 'Is there any racing on Wednesday?'

'Most definitely.' Hugh gave her a crinkly-eyed smile, his eyes sharing her amusement. 'Shall I call you with the arrangements?'

'All right.' She gave him one of her business cards. 'I'll look forward to it.'

'So will I,' he said warmly.

Waving a hand in farewell, he walked away. He didn't walk like Calum—he had a far more purposeful stride. Catching herself comparing again, Elaine told herself off angrily. There had been no word from Calum so it was perfectly obvious that he didn't want to know her any more.

So forget him; put him out of your mind; look forward to the future—don't get wistful about the past, she told herself. Look forward to this outing with Hugh—she wouldn't call it a date—and decide what you're going to wear—a far more important and pleasurable subject.

But when Elaine went into the office the next day she found a letter that had come via the fax machine. It was from the House of Brodey, asking her company to do the catering for the bicentennial celebrations on the island of Madeira in two months' time.

She dithered over accepting the commission for some time. It would be good for business, of course; her company's services came high and Brodey's had paid promptly the last time. Also, word had started to go round that she could cater for events lasting for several days, and more enquiries along those lines were starting to come in. To turn down the Madeira celebrations might have the reverse effect.

However, Elaine was willing to forgo all this if it meant Calum behaving towards her with the icy contempt of which she was quite sure he was capable. But if he felt like that surely he wouldn't have offered her the job? On the other hand, he might not even be there; he might leave the celebrations on the island in the hands of his cousin who lived there—Lennox Brodey.

Her thoughts in a whirl, Elaine was still undecided when Francesca rang a couple of days later, wanting to know why she hadn't heard from her.

'It's rather short notice,' Elaine prevaricated. 'I'm not sure that we can fit it in.'

'But you must. We couldn't possibly have anyone else to do it. You made such a marvellous job of all the parties in Oporto,' Francesca flattered. 'Promise me you will. I can't manage alone.'

'Will you be there?'

'Of course. And I'll help all I can.'

'How about the rest of your family?' Elaine asked, trying to keep her tone casual. 'Will they all be going?'

'I'm not sure,' Francesca answered on a careful note, probably guessing full well that she was only interested in Calum. 'Chris's parents definitely, so Chris will probably go as well. And Grandfather, of course.' Her tone became earnest. 'Please accept the job, Elaine. We really want you to.'

That 'we' could mean anything, but it pushed Elaine into saying, 'All right, Francesca. And thanks for the commission. I'll fax an acceptance through. Phone me again when you have more details.'

So now she was committed, although there was no guarantee that she would see Calum in Madeira. But even so Elaine's heart lifted and she was filled with an inner anticipation that would surface at the oddest moments, bringing a glow that lit her face and made her beautiful.

She went to the races with Hugh Steventon, met his sister, who was nice, and was invited to see her stables the following week—with Hugh, of course. Elaine also became friendly with some women of her own age at the health club and was invited out to a party one of them was having. There she met a divorced man with whom she got along well. At the end of the evening he asked for her phone number. Full of her new confidence, Elaine gave it to him and had no hesitation in accepting when he rang the following day and asked her out to the theatre.

From having a social life that was almost non-existent, Elaine now found that she had difficulty in finding the time to fit all the dates into her busy life. But it was fun and she was enjoying herself; it was pleasant to be admired, to go to new places and meet new people. With her revamped wardrobe, slimmer figure and new hairstyle, she felt rather like a brand-new doll that had just been taken out of its box. The only drawback was that the man who had brought the doll to life didn't want her any more. Like a spoilt child he had played with the toy and then got angry with it, tossing it aside. Calum's reaction still puzzled her, but she pushed the problem to the back of her mind and just tried to concentrate on enjoying herself. She would have succeeded—if only she could stop comparing every man she met with Calum.

About a month after her return to England, Elaine was at the office, seated at her desk and writing out cheques to cover a small pile of bills. It was quite late in the afternoon, bars of sunlight from the windows lying across the big room, a period when the place was fairly quiet, the phone calls made and the letters written.

Her secretary had already left and Elaine was working swiftly, wanting to get the job done because Hugh was coming to the office to collect her; they were going to drive to a concert in a stately home outside London, afterwards having supper at a restaurant on the way back. He would be on time, she knew; Hugh was never late, and they would arrive at the concert and the restaurant at just the right time. He was meticulous about arrangements, just as she was in her work. She supposed they complemented each other; Hugh certainly seemed to think so and he was becoming quite flatteringly attentive.

Her other boyfriend—she could think of no other way to describe them—was more laid-back, took her to less high-brow places, but in some ways was more fun to go out with. But of the two she somewhat preferred Hugh, and she loved going to his sister's stables, where she had been promised a ride on her next visit.

The office was on the first floor of a small modern block and had a mottled-glass panel in the door. There was the sound of footsteps ascending the steps outside and then a man's shadow showed through the glass and stopped at the door. Elaine looked at her watch, surprised that Hugh was so early. She hurried to finish the cheque she was writing and didn't look up as he came in.

'Hey, you're early! Be with you in a minute. I just have to finish——' Some tension in the air reached her and she glanced up, then became very still, the smile of welcome dying on her face. It was Calum who stood just within the doorway, his eyes fixed on her intently.

For a moment she was too stunned by surprise to react, then she felt a flush of colour creep up her cheeks. She looked away, to the pen she was holding, carefully putting it down, making sure it was exactly in line with the cheque-book, before she raised her eyes to him again.

'Hello, Elaine.'

She nodded. 'Calum.'

He hesitated, finally said, 'How are you?'

She had been expecting anything but such a mundane question. Beginning to feel angry, she said shortly, 'Fine.'

His eyes seemed to search her face then he too looked away for a moment before saying stiltedly, 'It's good to see you again.'

'Is it?' She saw his jaw tighten but before he could speak she said quickly, 'Have you come about your party in Madeira? I've been in frequent contact with Francesca and it's as advanced as we can be at this stage. Perhaps you'd like to see the folder.'

She got up to go to the filing-cabinet but he reached out and caught her wrist as she pulled the drawer open. 'I'm not interested in the party. It's you I came to see.'

Elaine gave him a wary glance. 'Why?'

'I—needed to see you again.'

Pulling her wrist free from his hold, she shut the drawer and stepped away from him. Dressed for the concert, she was wearing a red suit with a skirt much shorter than she used to wear. Her legs, long and shapely, were clad in sheer stockings, she wore high-heeled shoes, and her hair, although drawn back at the sides, hung softly to her shoulders.

'You look—different,' Calum said, his eyes lingering over her.

Remembering that it was he who had made the difference to her, Elaine's eyes softened a little. She felt a stir of emotion, began to feel excited that he had come so far just to see her. 'When did you get to England?' she asked.

'This morning. I had to go to Manchester on business, then came on here.'

'I see.' Her face tightened and she took a firm grip of her emotions. 'Just why have you come here, Calum?'

'Perhaps we could talk over dinner. I know a good——'

'I already have a date,' she interrupted tersely.

He frowned. 'Couldn't you break it?'

'No. Why should I alter my arrangements just because you take it into your head to turn up here?'

His mouth drew into a thin line. 'I have to get back to Portugal tomorrow. Are you sure you couldn't break it?'

'Couldn't you have phoned?' she countered.

'I very much want to see you,' he said steadily, his eyes holding hers.

She grew still, her heart beginning to race again. 'Why?'

'I've—missed you.'

A rush of longing made her suddenly ache for him, and memories of his lovemaking filled her mind, but somehow she fought them down, still wary. 'I hope you received my note thanking you for the flowers?' she said in a clipped voice.

'Yes—I did.'

There was something in his tone that made her shoot him a sharp glance. 'They were beautiful; did you choose them yourself?' she probed.

A grim, rueful kind of look came into Calum's grey eyes. 'I didn't send them. They were from my grandfather.'

'But it was your name on the——' She broke off, realising that both men bore the same name. 'I see,' she said coldly. So he hadn't attempted to contact her in any way in all these weeks. And now he'd just walked in and expected her to change all her plans to suit him. Her heart hardening, Elaine sat on the edge of her desk and folded her arms. She gave an ironical laugh. 'Oh, sure, you must really have missed me.'

He took a step towards her, but the fiery look she gave him stopped him from reaching out to touch her. Instead he thrust his hands into his pockets. 'I want to talk to you, Elaine. I thought we could spend the evening together.'

'I've already told you, I have a date and——' She broke off, her eyes widening. 'My God, is that what you've come here for? For someone to spend the night with?' She got to her feet, furious. 'Am I supposed to make myself available to you whenever you happen to have an odd night to spend in London? Is that it? A way to while away the time?'

'No, I——'

But Elaine's temper was completely lost. 'And you had the nerve to walk out on me because you said I'd used you! What the hell do you think this is? Or is it all right for a man to use a woman but not the other way round? You chauvinist! You arrogant, conceited——'

Striding across to her, Calum took hold of her shoulders. 'That isn't why I came! Listen to me.' She went to argue so he gave her an angry shake. 'I said, listen to me.'

'No, I won't damn well listen.' Putting her hands against his chest, she tried to push him away. 'I suppose you have a woman waiting for you to turn up wherever you go: New York, Hong Kong, Madeira. Well, don't expect me to be your London lay-over, because I've got better things to do and I——'

Losing his own temper, Calum exclaimed, 'Damn you, Elaine! Shut up!' And, dragging her to him, he kissed her fiercely.

If he had taken her in his arms and kissed her when he'd first walked in, things might have been very different, but now Elaine was too angry to let the instantaneous rush of longing engulf her. She fought the whirlpool, stiffened her body, resisted desire. Her lips stayed firmly closed and when Calum at last raised his head he found her eyes still open and glaring into his with shrivelling contempt.

'If you have anything to say then say it and go,' she bit out coldly.

He stared down at her for a long moment, his hands still on her shoulders, a tense, strangely shocked look in his eyes. He went to say something, stopped, then, 'Your date,' he said unsteadily. 'A man?'

'Of course.'

She felt a tremor of emotion go through the hands that gripped her. 'Do you go to bed with him?'

Pushing him violently away, she said furiously, 'Get out of here! Get out of my office. How dare you ask me such a question? Who the hell do you think you are? You have no right to——'

Calum caught her wrist as she raised her arm to hit him. His face taut with emotion, he said, 'I have the right because I——'

He broke off as there was a sharp rap on the glass of the door-panel. They both swung round and caught sight of someone standing outside, then the door opened and Hugh walked in.

Calum instantly let her go and turned away, fighting to recover his self-control. Elaine put a hand to her face, covering her flushed cheeks.

Hugh looked swiftly from one to the other of them, then said sharply, 'Elaine? Are you all right?'

'Y-yes, of course.' She took a deep breath. 'This— this is a client. He was just leaving.'

Calum gave her a scorching glance, then turned and let his eyes run over Hugh. He gave a small, contemptuous smile, then his head came up in arrogant pride and he strode out of the office.

Neither of them moved as they heard Calum's footsteps running down the stairs; only when the front door of the building had slammed shut behind him did Elaine slowly relax and let out a long breath.

'Who was that?' Hugh demanded.

'A client,' she repeated mechanically, her mind still on Calum.

'Do you usually row like that with all your clients?' he said drily.

She blinked and licked lips gone dry, tasted Calum's kiss on her mouth. 'No, of course not.' She turned away. 'I won't be a moment; I must put these things away.' She bundled the cheque-book and bills into the safe anyhow, then picked up her bag, aware that she must look a mess. 'If you'll excuse me, I'll tidy up first.'

Elaine went to go to the door but Hugh put out an arm to stop her. Looking at her face, he said, 'He kissed you.' She didn't deny it, and he said urgently, 'Who was he, Elaine?'

Sighing, she put down her bag and faced him. 'An old flame.'

Hugh's eyes narrowed. 'A lover?'

She met his gaze steadily. 'Yes.'

'It didn't look as if you parted very amicably.' She didn't speak and he said, 'When did you break up?'

'Not very long ago. But I didn't know he was coming here today. I—I didn't expect to see him again.'

'What did he want?'

'To take me out to dinner tonight.'

'But you refused?'

'Of course. I have a date with you.'

He seemed pleased by that, but said, 'Was that all he wanted?'

'I didn't enquire,' Elaine answered, her voice becoming cool at this interrogation. 'Excuse me.'

She went out to the cloakroom to comb her hair, but found herself gazing at her reflection without seeing it. What had Calum really wanted? What had he come to say that he hadn't got round to saying in the end? And had that been jealousy in his face when he'd asked her if she was going to bed with Hugh? It had certainly been in Hugh's face when he'd asked her almost the same question about Calum.

Elaine sighed. Men and their egos, their sensitive pride! She felt a flash of anger. How dared Calum walk in here and just expect her to fall into bed with him again? He should have phoned first, she thought crossly.

That brought a leap of surprised laughter to her eyes. Would she really have broken her date with Hugh and gone to bed with Calum again if she'd known he was coming to London? She pushed the thought aside because Hugh was waiting and there was no time to dwell on it now.

But later, at the concert, Elaine's attention strayed from the music, back to that all-important question. And the answer now was clear in her mind, so overwhelmingly clear that it shocked her. She knew, quite definitely, that if Calum had rung first she would have been with him now, making love in her bed, instead of sitting at this tedious concert. Her body ached to be with him, to be a part of him, yearned to know the excitement of his caresses again. Closing her eyes, she could almost feel the touch of his hands, gentle yet overwhelmingly erotic as they explored her. His lips...

She moved restlessly and felt Hugh glance at her questioningly. From somewhere she managed to smile at him. Reaching out, he took her hand and held it in his for the rest of the performance.

They stopped for supper at an inn on the outskirts of a small town, a pseudo-medieval place with beams and an ingle-nook fireplace. The décor might have been artificial but the food was genuinely good. Hugh was attentive and entertaining and Elaine tried to be amusing and animated in return, but once Hugh flicked his fingers in front of her face and said, 'Hey, come back to me.'

Elaine blinked. 'Oh! Sorry. My mind wandered for a moment.'

Hugh's mouth twisted ruefully. 'Not for the first time tonight. And I need hardly ask where. Your ex-boyfriend, I suppose. If he is an ex?'

'Oh, yes. Definitely.' Elaine said it reassuringly, but she rather thought she was reassuring herself.

'Did your affair with him last very long?'

'No.' You could hardly call two or three days an affair, she thought wryly.

'But it was intense.'

Elaine frowned and looked up at him. 'Why do you say that?'

'When I walked in on you, you were having quite a row. People don't row unless their emotions are involved. Don't you agree?'

It was an aspect that hadn't occurred to Elaine before. There had been passion between them at the *quinta*, of course, but it had been physical passion, not emotional. Then they had parted in anger. But, remembering Calum's behaviour towards her that afternoon, Elaine realised that the atmosphere had indeed been charged with deep feelings. He hadn't come in anger, but it had grown, and when he'd kissed her... She looked away, frowning, uncertain, and quickly changed the subject.

For the rest of the evening she made sure that Hugh didn't have to complain again, but when he drove her back to her flat she hesitated a moment before asking him in for a coffee.

Her flat was on the top floor of a large terraced house in Westbourne Grove, small and therefore quite cheap, because she'd put most of her money into starting the business. It wasn't the first time that Hugh had been there. He'd called for her a couple of times and she'd asked him back for coffee once before. It hadn't led to anything, because it had been too soon, but they had been going out together for some weeks now and she sensed that their relationship had reached the stage when they could become lovers. Hugh, she knew, wanted this but hadn't rushed her, and, until today, she had been ready for it too, had even been anticipating it with some eagerness. But now she felt strangely reluctant.

Elaine leading the way, they climbed the many stairs to her door. When they got inside Hugh immediately took her in his arms and kissed her. He knew how to kiss, and it was warm and sensuous, a pleasurable experience. She responded, but soon broke away. 'I'll make the coffee,' she said with a smile.

But Hugh pulled her back into his arms. 'Aren't we adult enough to forget that silly excuse?'

When he kissed her for the second time, Elaine put her arms round his neck and tried to return it as avidly as he, but somehow there was no excitement there; the anticipation and eagerness had entirely gone.

His hand went to the opening of her blouse, slid inside. Closing her eyes tightly, she tried to lose herself in his embrace, expecting any second to experience the same yearning that had engulfed her when Calum had caressed her. But it was just a hand that touched her; it evoked no desire, no gasping need. Hugh's touch was alien, something to be endured instead of eagerly longed for. She did her best but Hugh sensed her inner withdrawal and raised his head. He gave a short laugh. 'I've an idea I'm wasting my time.'

There was no point in denying it. 'I'm sorry.'

'Whoever that ex-boyfriend of yours is, I'd like to punch him on the nose. We were getting along fine until he came back on the scene.' Putting his hands on her arms, Hugh looked at her steadily. 'Is there any hope for us, Elaine?'

She shrugged helplessly. 'I just don't know. I was so pleased when I met you. I like you so much. But now...'

'But it isn't there, is it?'

'No.' She shook her head. 'I'm sorry. I—didn't expect it to be like this. I wanted to be—closer to you. But...' Again she shrugged. 'I didn't expect to ever see him again. I haven't been thinking about him that much. If he hadn't come to the office today...'

Lifting a finger, Hugh put it against her lips. 'Hush. You don't have to explain. I understand. Old loves can play the devil with the emotions.'

'I wasn't in love with him,' Elaine said quickly.

He looked at her for a moment, then gave a regretful sigh. 'I should have known that someone as beautiful as you wouldn't be heart-free.'

'But I am. I——' She broke off, flushed.

'I'd better go. Goodnight, Elaine.'

'Will I see you again?' she asked unhappily.

'Perhaps. If you are ever really free again.'

He let himself out and she didn't go with him. Sitting down on the settee, she realised an unpalatable truth: that Calum had taught her how wonderful physical love could be, but had done so with such skill that he had forever spoiled it for her with other men. When you had tasted perfection, how could you possibly take the risk of anything less with anyone else? In a few weeks she had gone from being completely afraid of sex to knowing the glory of fulfilment and back to being afraid of sex again in case it should turn out to be mundane.

So where did that leave her?

But it hadn't been like that before today, she knew. She could have gone on being happy in her new-found sexuality, have gone to bed with Hugh and enjoyed it, but something had happened today. Even though she had resisted him when Calum had kissed her, there had been such feeling, such intensity in his kiss, in the way he'd dragged her into his arms, not brooking any denial. The memory of it made Elaine catch her breath. She had been so angry that she hadn't realised at the time, but now she saw again the fierceness in his face, the craving in his eyes. Remembered, too, the stunned expression on his face when she had resisted him. Maybe no other woman had rejected him before; perhaps that was why. And she was pretty certain that no woman had ever thrown him out before, either.

Well, he'd had a damn cheek just walking in the way he had. She'd had a right to be angry. And she was even more angry with Calum now because he had spoiled it for her with Hugh. Hugh was nice and she liked him; it wasn't his fault that he hadn't set her senses on fire, hadn't even awakened them at all.

The phone rang, breaking into her thoughts. Mechanically she picked up the receiver and said the number.

'Elaine?' Calum's voice brought her to tingling alertness.

It was a moment before she said, 'Yes?' on an unsteady note.

'I want to come up and see you.'

'What makes you think I'm alone?' she prevaricated.

'I saw him go.'

She caught her breath. 'Where are you?'

'In my car. You can see it if you look out of the window.'

Putting down the receiver, she went to the window and parted the curtains. Down in the dark chasm of the street a car flashed its lights. She looked down at it for a moment. So he expected her just to say yes and he'd come up and get into bed with her, did he?

Picking up the phone again, she said clearly, 'Go to hell!' and slammed it down.

It was less than two minutes before the phone rang again. Elaine let it ring several times before she picked up the receiver. Before he could speak, she said, 'The main door's open. Hurry! I *want* you.'

CHAPTER EIGHT

THE door of the flat was standing open. Calum walked through and looked round but Elaine wasn't there. Closing the door, he strode through the sitting-room into the bedroom. She was waiting for him, naked, the soft curves of her body lit and shadowed by the soft light of the bedside lamp. He gave a great gasp, and stood still for a moment to gaze his fill; the next he stepped forward and caught her up in his arms.

'Elaine! Elaine.' He said her name on a shuddering sigh of excitement that was lost as she sought greedily for his lips.

They kissed hungrily, taking each other's mouth in hot, biting eagerness, already panting with fierce desire. But then Elaine's hands were on his clothes, fumbling with his tie, the buttons of his shirt.

Calum gave a low, hoarse groan. 'Oh, God, I've missed you. I've missed you.' Still trying to kiss her, he struggled out of his jacket, kicked off his shoes.

Her hands were at the buckle of his belt, unfastening it, pulling down his zip, loosing him from the constraints of his clothes, setting his manhood free. She touched him, her fingers soft but avid in their caresses, and he gave a great cry of tormented pleasure. Putting his hands low on her hips, he held her against himself and cried out again as she moved her body voluptuously, delighting in driving them both into a frenzy of excitement. Calum drew her to him, raining fervent kisses on her throat, her eyes, her mouth. 'Elaine, my darling.'

His voice was thick, uncontrolled, the ache of need deep in his throat.

'I want you,' she said against his mouth, then broke away to move her body against the length of his. She felt shuddering tremors of awareness run through him, heard his gasping moans of exquisite anticipation, felt the hammer-beat of his heart under her hand, the hot sweat of perspiration on his skin. Her own aching need for him suddenly engulfed her. She held her body hard against his, wanting him, *wanting him*. 'Now!' she cried out. 'Take me now!'

The bed was only two feet away. With a groan, Calum laid her on it, and the next second was taking her with passionate, tempestuous abandon, taking her with a hunger so urgent that it was wild and uncontrolled, almost savage in its primitiveness. At that moment they had no name, no country, no status—they were simply a man and a woman who needed each other desperately, and who found in the other's body the most sublime pleasure they had ever known. Their lovemaking lifted them to the heights of ecstasy, a place where angels sang a triumphant song, and for a few moments there was heaven on earth. A place one was tremendously reluctant to leave but was humbly grateful for having seen.

Calum was slumped against her, his heart still beating loudly in his chest, his hair clinging damply to his forehead. Feeling something digging into her, Elaine looked and realised that it was one of his cuff-links, still in the sleeve of his shirt, which he hadn't had time to take off. She gave a low chuckle and he opened his eyes, lifted an eyebrow,

'You still have some of your clothes on.'

He kissed her, then sat up to take off his shirt, kick off his other things. Then he grinned at her. 'I haven't been that eager to make love in years.'

'When was the last time?'

'The last time I couldn't wait to take my clothes off? I don't know. Never, probably.' Propping himself up on his elbow, he caressed her breasts, then bent to kiss them. When he raised his head, his eyes suddenly serious, he said, 'If you hadn't let me in, I think I would have beaten the door down. I've been going through hell all evening, knowing you were with somebody else, wondering if you would end up in bed with him.'

Elaine sat up, slipped between the covers. Not looking at him, she said, 'I had intended to let him make love to me tonight.'

Calum's hand had been stroking her arm, but it grew still. 'Why didn't you?'

'You know why.'

'I want to hear you say it.'

She looked at him over her shoulder, her hair soft on her back. 'You came.'

'At just the right moment, it seems.'

Her voice hardened a little. 'Or the wrong moment.'

'Never that.' Sitting up, Calum leaned against the headboard and put his hands on her shoulders from behind her. Gently he massaged them, his hands warm and strong. 'Don't you want to know why I came back?'

'You said you were over here on business.'

'That was merely a sop to my pride in case you told me to go to hell.'

'Which I did.'

'Which you did,' he agreed, and kissed her shoulder. 'But it was merely an excuse; I needed to see you again.'

'For—this, I suppose.'

'This, yes, if the fates were kind. But I wanted to tell you how much I've missed you, how often I've thought about you and wanted to be with you again.'

She was silent for a moment, then said, 'I didn't expect ever to see you again.'

'No.' His hand stilled on her shoulder. 'I was a fool, wasn't I? But back in Portugal I had begun to hope that you—cared about me. It came as rather a shock to find out that you looked on me as nothing more than a holiday affair.'

Frowning a little, she said carefully, 'I thought that was all you would want from me; that the last thing you would want was for me to get emotionally involved, to be possessive.'

'That's what I thought, too, until the storm. Until we really made love. It was so incredibly wonderful, then—and every time afterwards.'

At that she twisted round to give him a surprised look. 'Isn't it always like that for you, then? With every woman you go with?'

Calum gave a gasping laugh. 'No, my sweet innocent, it is not always like that. Far from it. How could you think it was?'

'I just thought that you were incredibly good at it,' she admitted naïvely.

'I am, of course,' he said with tongue-in-cheek vanity, which earned him a dig in the ribs. 'But it takes two, you know. And you, my lovely one, are sensational.'

'Am I?' She gave a pleased smile, then, instinctively knowing the time was right, said, 'My husband always said that I was frigid.'

'He was a fool,' Calum said brusquely. 'Was that why you were so afraid, the first time?'

She nodded and, looking down at her hands, said, 'I was a virgin when I married him. He wasn't—gentle or patient, like you. He thought only of his own pleasure, and he made me do things that revolted me. When I— I just couldn't, he used to shout at me and call me a cold, frigid bitch. It got so that every time I got rigid with fright, but that only made it worse, of course. Sometimes it made me physically ill.' She paused, then said, 'Sometimes he made me drunk so that I would be relaxed and he could do what he wanted.'

'The bastard,' Calum swore under his breath. 'Did he beat you?'

'He didn't take a stick to me or anything, but sometimes he would lose his temper and hit me, and he was always rough; he liked to be rough.' She paused and then said contemplatively, 'Maybe he liked me to be tense because it gave him an excuse to hurt me. Maybe that was what gave him his kicks, because he kept taking me. And perhaps it was only when I learned that it was easier just to lie there that he started to go with other women.'

'Why didn't you leave him?'

'I was very much in love with him when we married. I was very young, you see. And for a long time I thought it was all my fault; he made me feel like that. I thought there was something wrong with me and that I'd failed him, that I was ruining his life, as he said.

'He was away a lot, too, on courses and things, so that I had time to recover, and I always hoped it would be all right the next time he came home. My marriage vows meant a great deal to me, and there was a lot of parental pressure to stay with him. No one else knew, you see, because he was perfectly reasonable apart from bed. But towards the end I had begun to hate him, and I had started to make plans to leave when he was killed.'

'My poor darling, no wonder you were so uptight that first time.'

'You were right, though; I shouldn't have just—chosen you, to see if sex could be anything other than what I'd known with Neil.'

'Now that I know why, I'm very flattered that you did. You put a great deal of trust in me, I think.'

'But it wouldn't have worked, would it, if it hadn't been for the storm?'

Calum smiled and slipped his hands round her so that he could cup her breasts. 'Oh, I think we would have found a way. I sensed the latent fire in you and somehow I just knew that behind that prim and proper veneer there was a passionate, ardent woman just waiting to come out.'

Elaine smiled. 'I think she would have stayed locked away forever if it hadn't been for you. I'm very grateful to you, Calum. And I'm sorry that I hurt you.'

'I was an arrogant fool. I should have come here weeks ago. But it isn't pleasant to think that you've been used. Especially when——'

'No, I know,' she interrupted. 'I'm sorry.' She put her hands over his as they held her. 'But I'm not like Tiffany, really I'm not.'

'Do you think I didn't realise that the minute I came to my senses? I called you at the *quinta* the following day, but Senhora Varosa said that you'd already gone. It was then I convinced myself that you really didn't care——' He broke off, his voice thickening, to say, 'God, I wish I had a dozen hands.'

Elaine laughed richly. 'You work miracles with just two.'

'Let them go, then.'

'I kind of like them where they are.' Looking over her shoulder, she smiled at him provocatively. 'So will I be your London lay-over now?'

Looking into her warm, smiling green eyes, at her lovely face with its mass of red hair, Calum finally said what he had come to England to say. 'I was rather hoping you would be my wife.'

She began to laugh, but as she looked into his eyes the amusement slowly died from her face and her mouth parted in stunned astonishment as she stared at him. 'You're—you're not serious?' she said faintly.

His mouth twisted in tender chagrin. 'Haven't you been listening to me? Didn't you hear when I told you how devastated I was when I thought you didn't care? I love you, my darling, and I want to marry you.'

'But—but...'

He shook his head and put a finger over her lips. 'There are no buts.'

She blinked at that, then recovered a little and said, 'But I'm not blonde!'

Calum raised his eyes to heaven. 'That stupid tradition. What the hell has the colour of someone's hair got to do with falling in love?'

She was about to say that his family might well object to his breaking with tradition, and especially to his wanting to marry someone who was little more than a glorified cook, but she stayed silent. Calum was man enough to know his own mind and must already have realised that his family might object. The fact that it didn't worry him was tremendously flattering. But she felt compelled to say, 'Is this something that has just come into your mind, or have you thought about it before?'

His eyes caressing her, he said, 'It's what I came to England for—to ask you. When I left the *quinta* I was angry, and even more so when I found that you'd gone. But I couldn't get you out of my mind; my life felt empty and hollow. I've never felt like that before. No matter how hard I worked, how much I tried to fill my time, there was this great emptiness in my heart. I longed to hold you in my arms again, to touch you, kiss you.

'But it wasn't only for that. If something interesting happened I wanted to turn to you and tell you. I wanted to see your face light when you smiled, hear your laughter. I imagined you in every room of my house, but that only made the house seem empty too.'

She had let his hands go and he lifted one to gently stroke her face as she gazed at him with wonder in her eyes. 'I went back to the *quinta*,' Calum went on. 'God, how I hated myself then for having ruined everything, for having let you go. I spent hours just standing in my bedroom, the garden, on the boat, just remembering.'

'Why didn't you call me, or write?'

'I picked up the receiver a hundred times, but I knew that I'd made you angry, and I was afraid that you'd refuse to speak to me, let alone see me again, so I decided just to turn up.'

'I thought it was over. I thought you hated me.' There was a defensive note in her voice, but Calum didn't notice it.

'I needed to be sure of my own feelings before I came, before I asked you.' His fingertip ran sensuously over her lips. 'So, my darling Elaine, I've come to claim you for my own, to make you my wife.'

Elaine had been overwhelmed to hear that he loved her; it made her feel warm and happy and grateful. That a man such as Calum could love her when she'd spent so many years feeling like a misfit, unloved and ill-used, was a miracle in itself. She had missed him, too, and had wanted to be close to him again as much, it seemed, as he had needed her.

But whereas she had left his life empty, he had started hers anew. Until tonight she had thought that she could have a sexual relationship with any man she chose; it was only when it came to accepting Hugh's advances that she'd known she couldn't, not when Calum had come back and made it plain that he still wanted her. She only knew that there had been a chance to go to bed with Calum again and she had seized it, unable to resist. She had acted instinctively and there had been no time to think about the implications.

Now he wanted her to be his wife and, from the way he had phrased it, was fully confident that she would accept. He hadn't, in fact, actually asked her, had just said that he'd come to claim her. Perhaps it was that, perhaps it was also the way he'd just turned up out of the blue and expected her to take him back that made up her mind. It wasn't easy, not when she was in bed with him, not when he was looking at her so warmly, so lovingly, fully expecting her to say yes. But Elaine knew, for her own sake, what she had to do. So, drawing back, she shook her head. 'I don't think so.'

He gave a laughing frown. 'Don't think what?'

'That I want to marry you.'

His eyes widened incredulously as he stared at her.

'We could still see each other whenever you come to England, if you want to,' Elaine went on.

'No, that isn't what I want.' Calum sat up straight, his body tense. 'I want you for my wife. I want you to live with me and have my children. To be with me always.'

'Yes, I know.' Elaine looked at him steadily. 'You keep saying what *you* want. But have you bothered to think about what *I* might want?' Her voice hardened. 'And did you bother to think about how I might be feeling when you were busy sorting out your own feelings back in Portugal, and didn't even call me? I put you out of my life, Calum. I was starting to build something for myself, meeting new people and——'

'Like this man tonight,' Calum cut in grimly.

'Yes, like Hugh. He was introducing me to a whole new set of experiences. I was starting to have fun.' She paused, then said, 'I know you gave me the confidence to start living again, and I'm intensely grateful to you for——'

Calum made a sharp dismissive gesture. 'I don't want your gratitude.'

'I know that. But you can't just walk back into my life and expect me to completely change mine because you've made up your mind that you want to marry me.'

'If you loved me you would.'

She looked at him, saw the tension in his face, the disbelief in his eyes. Something pulled at her heart, but she ignored it and said deliberately, 'I don't know that I want to give up my whole life, everything I've worked for, just to fill an emptiness in yours.'

'I see.' Calum gave a short, mirthless laugh and lifted a hand to wipe it across his face. 'I must admit I never expected that answer. You're the only woman I've ever asked to marry me, the only woman I've ever wanted enough to——' He broke off. 'I'd better go.'

'You don't have to.'

'Oh, yes, I think I must.' And, getting out of bed, he began to dress, searching for his clothes where they'd fallen.

Elaine didn't watch him, but she said, 'We could still see each other.'

He rounded on her. 'I don't want a mistress,' he said on a note of harsh bitterness. 'I want you in my life, to be a part of me.'

'Then you must give me time to sort out *my* feelings,' she answered in a sudden spurt of honest anger.

Hope flared in his eyes. 'What are you saying?'

'You didn't ask me how I felt about you. You just took it for granted that I loved you enough to marry you. Work it out for yourself. I *don't know*.'

'Elaine.'

He came towards her, his face intent, but she shook her head. 'No. Goodnight, Calum.' He still hesitated and she said, 'Just go away. I need to think.'

'All right.' But he bent to kiss her lingeringly and, as he raised his head, said with new strength in his voice, 'I love you, Elaine. And I won't give up until you say yes.'

From that day on Elaine experienced what it was like to be wooed. An old-fashioned word but the only one she could find to describe the flowers and gifts, the phone calls and the letters which were showered upon her. Calum went back to Portugal but there wasn't a day that went by when he didn't find some way of letting her know that he hadn't given up. He even came over to England again, but was thunderstruck when she wouldn't let him make love to her.

'You said you didn't want me for your mistress,' she reminded him.

'I still don't, but that doesn't mean we can't——'

'So why are you complaining?' she cut in.

Folding his arms, Calum gave her a narrow-eyed look. 'I've an idea that you're punishing me.'

'No—but maybe you're learning something.'

'And just how long do you intend to hold me at arm's length?'

Elaine smiled, mischief in her green eyes, and had no idea how lovely she looked at that moment and why Calum caught his breath. 'You'll just have to wait and see, won't you?'

'Don't tell me you don't want it, because I know you do,' he said raggedly.

Resting her hands on his shoulders and looking up into his eyes, she said, 'Of course I do. Desperately. But it has to be this way. It has to do with—integrity.'

He had no choice but to accept her terms, even though they were both driven crazy with frustration at times— most of the time. It was especially hard when they met again in Madeira. Elaine flew in with Ned, Malcolm and a couple of other assistants. The first celebration, for people in the wine trade, was to be held at a hotel in Funchal, and all her helpers had been booked to stay there, but Francesca told Elaine that she was to stay at the family house, known all over Madeira as the Brodey estate, a couple of miles outside the town. It was a beautiful house, gabled and white-walled, slumbering in a typically English-style garden, only this garden had arum lilies growing wild, and clumps of brilliant bird-of-paradise flowers near the stream that cascaded through it.

A few hours later Calum flew into the island and he too came to stay at the house, along with Sam Gallagher who was over from America. There were several other people around when he and Elaine met, so they merely exchanged polite greetings, and the house was so full, and everyone so busy, that there was little opportunity for them to be alone. Francesca hadn't known Sam was coming; it seemed that Calum had deliberately invited him behind her back, and she was in a turmoil about it—one minute angry, the next excited. Luckily, this meant she was too absorbed in her own feelings to notice the tension between Calum and Elaine.

The first dinner went off successfully, and the following night there was to be a huge party in a marquee on the lawn of the house. Elaine, her more sober clothes left at home, put on a dress with a figure-hugging top in green velvet and a skirt that burst out into rich and riotous greens and reds and gold: a jewel-box of colours.

She went into the marquee early, to make sure that everything was exactly right: the flowers that swathed the wooden poles and adorned the tables, the crystal glassware, the shining cutlery, the waiters in their immaculate uniforms. It wasn't really necessary because Ned had already seen to it all, but he liked her praise, which she gave warmly, and it delighted them both to see their art brought to perfection.

Calum entered the marquee with the rest of his family, ready to greet their guests. Elaine was standing at the far side of the great tent and he came straight over to her. Regardless of everyone else, he took her hands in his and raised them to his lips. She flushed a little, but didn't look away from the longing and the love in his eyes.

'How beautiful you look. Do you know what I wish for, more than anything in the world? The one thing that would make this moment the most perfect in my life?' She didn't answer and he said, 'To take you over to my grandfather now and tell him that we're engaged. To announce it tonight to everyone here so that they can all see how lucky I am, how much I love you.'

She gave a small laugh. 'I'm not sure whether that comes under moral blackmail or coercion. But I don't think it's playing fair.'

'I just wish it had worked,' he said with a frustrated sigh. 'Be very careful, because I'm fast getting to the stage when I could easily kidnap you and hold you prisoner until you say yes.'

Francesca and Sam left the party early, so didn't see Calum insist on dancing three times with Elaine.

'People will notice,' she admonished him.

'Good. I have no wish to hide how I feel about you.'

She gave him a troubled look, then said, 'Tomorrow—could we talk?'

'Of course.' But he frowned a little, worry in his eyes, his supreme self-confidence already having been shaken and open now to another blow.

She was very busy most of the next day, seeing to the dismantling of the marquee and checking tradesmen's bills, so it was late in the afternoon before she was able to get away.

Calum hadn't sought her out, perhaps reluctant to hear what she had to say, so she went to look for him and found him in the old chapel in the grounds.

'What a lovely little place!' she exclaimed as she walked in and saw the plain white altar and decorated ceiling.

'It was,' Calum said ruefully. 'But the roof has leaked and pulled part of the plasterwork down in that corner.'

'Don't you use the place, then?'

'No. It's too small for grand family occasions like weddings and funerals, although Stella has said that she'd like her child to be christened here, if it's possible. It would take quite a lot to repair it, though.'

'Can the House of Brodey afford it?'

'Oh, I should think so,' he said, watching her. 'But for just one christening ceremony?'

'I'm quite sure that Stella will have lots of children,' Elaine said firmly. 'So I think you should go ahead and repair it.'

'Very well.'

She gave him a slightly surprised look, not having expected him to agree so swiftly. What she read in his face made her suddenly aware that she could ask anything of him and he would give it to her. That, too, was disconcerting. Turning abruptly, she walked outside and waited for him to join her.

They walked together in silence down one of the paths, cobbled in a regular pattern and edged with neat, short box hedges, the borders full of flowers, until they came to a stone seat under a gnarled old tree. Elaine stopped, and turned to face him. Calum had his hands thrust into his pockets and his face was taut with tension.

'I asked you to give me time to think,' Elaine began. 'I have to admit, I haven't thought of much else. And I've missed you. But——' Hope had flared in his eyes, but was quickly dampened. 'But I want to be honest with you. You see, after Neil had been so cruel to me, when he died, I vowed that I'd never marry again, never place myself in a position where I could be so hurt and abused by another man. Not just physically, but mentally and emotionally, too.' Reading his mind, she gave a small smile and said, 'Yes, I know you're not like that. That I would be—safe with you.'

She paused and picked a flower from a nearby bed, twisted its stem in her fingers. 'But in the three years I've been alone I've come to value my freedom, my independence, and my ability to found and run a business successfully. I know that compared to your business empire mine is of very little importance——' she raised earnest eyes to his '—but to me it means a great deal. I know that if I married you you would want me to give it up, but I would find that very hard to do. I would be willing to compromise, to take on a partner perhaps, so that it wouldn't be a full-time occupation.'

Calum went to speak but she quickly put her fingers over his lips. 'No, please hear me out.'

Putting his hand over hers, he kissed her fingers one by one. 'What else?'

'It's a matter of trust, I suppose. I trusted Neil and he let me down, not once, but again and again. I only found out fully after he was dead, but he'd been unfaithful to me with a great many women, some in quite long affairs, others just one-night stands. It destroyed my trust in him, in love, and to a great extent in men too. I expect that's difficult for you to understand, but it was the way I felt.'

She paused, perhaps expecting him to make some protest, but Calum stayed silent, and she went on with some difficulty, 'I know that you're—experienced. But then, men have to be, don't they? And I know that now, at this moment, you love me and don't want anyone else. But if I married you and then found out that, some time in the future, you had—betrayed my trust, then I don't think that I could bear it.'

'My darling girl. Yes, I *do* love you, with all my heart. What can I say to——?'

But she interrupted quickly, saying, 'No, I don't want you to say anything, not right now. Now it's your turn to think about it. Because when you asked me to marry you you were quite sure that I would give up everything and be the kind of wife you wanted, expected. But I need a degree of independence, to be my own person, not just Calum Brodey's wife. And you have to make up your mind if that's enough for you, if you could live with it without coercing me to change. If you can, then I'll happily marry you. Because I love you, Calum, and I would always, *always* be faithful to you. You would be able to trust me, as I must be able to trust you.'

She got to her feet. 'I'm going back to the house to pack now, and I'm catching an evening flight home. Promise me that you'll take your time. Don't let——' she smiled a little '—shall we call it your libido? rule your head. I'll be in London. And please don't send me any more presents.' Bending, she kissed his lips lingeringly. 'Goodbye, Calum.'

When she reached the end of the path, Elaine glanced back. Calum was still sitting on the seat, gazing after her, his expression unreadable, but he didn't wave, just watched as she walked away.

The presents stopped, as she'd asked, but so too did his daily calls. She had mixed feelings about this, was partly glad that he wasn't trying to coerce her, but began to think that maybe he had given up on her altogether. So it was a relief to get a letter from him saying that Stella had had her baby and that he was taking over from Lennox in Madeira for a while. He didn't mention that he was still thinking about her ultimatum, but then, he didn't have to—she knew he would be thinking about nothing else, as she had done.

From Madeira he went back to Oporto and she didn't hear from him for some time. Then, one late summer evening, she walked out of her office in its quiet back-street, and found him waiting for her.

'Calum!' Her face lit up with surprised joy at seeing him.

'Hello, Elaine.' He smiled at her. 'Will you marry me? On any terms you——'

But Elaine had dropped her briefcase to run into his arms and fling her own round his neck. 'Oh, yes! I've missed you so much.'

He kissed her deeply, almost desperately, and said against her mouth, 'I can't live without you, my darling. Marry me soon, soon.'

They went back to her flat and made love, passionately, fiercely, making up for all the weeks they'd been apart. But all too soon Calum had to leave again; he was on his way to New York, to 'try and sort out Chris and Tiffany' as he put it.

'Francesca has been there too; I had a postcard from her. But she didn't mention Sam. Hasn't she seen him since they had that row in Madeira?'

'I don't think so. But she's seen Chris and she's worried about him. It was she who asked me to go and try to help him.'

'Maybe he's in love with Tiffany,' Elaine mused. She looked at Calum, not having to say that love was a force to be reckoned with.

'But is she in love with him, or is she using him as we fear?' He kissed her, greatly reluctant to leave. 'When I finish in New York I'll take you back to Portugal with me and tell Grandfather that we're engaged. I can't announce it officially until then. But in the meantime——' he took a small box from his pocket '—will you wear this for me, my love? It isn't the official Brodey betrothal ring—Grandfather has that in the bank—but this is one my father gave to my mother and which she always wore.'

He put the solitaire diamond on the third finger not of her left hand, but of her right, reserving the traditional place for his family ring, she realised. But it was at that moment that Elaine felt really engaged, really committed. 'I'll wear it with love, and pride,' she said huskily, her eyes full of both.

It was nearly two weeks before she saw Calum again. At first, from New York, he called every day but then, unaccountably, the calls suddenly stopped. Worried, Elaine called his New York office but was told that he was busy. Then he turned up on her doorstep again.

'You'll have to stop doing this to me,' she complained laughingly. 'My poor heart can't stand it.'

He didn't respond and when he came into the flat she saw that he looked tired; but there was something more than that; he looked—dejected.

'What is it? Is it your grandfather? Or Chris?' she asked in concern.

'No.' He shook his head. 'Something's happened. Something that concerns all of us, I suppose, but particularly Francesca and me.'

A sudden fear made her heart go cold. He looked so serious. Instinctively she knew that it concerned her too. 'Would you like a drink?'

He nodded and sat down in the armchair. Usually when he came they sat together on the settee, and somehow his choosing the armchair made it seem as if he was distancing himself from her.

He took a long drink, then said, 'We keep some private papers in the safe in the family flat in New York. Somehow Tiffany got hold of them and she's written an article about what she found. She's disappeared, but we presume that she's sold it to a gossip magazine and that it will come out at any time. It could cause quite a nasty scandal.'

She felt herself go white. 'About you and Francesca?' she said hollowly.

'What?' He looked startled. 'No! Not the two of us together. Not that. Francesca fell in love with a student when she was at college, was nuts about him. Grandfather realised he wasn't right for her and used me as a go-between to buy him off. The paper he signed guaranteeing never to see her again was taken from the safe.'

'That wasn't so very terrible,' Elaine said.

'Perhaps not, but Francesca never knew about it. She went slightly crazy when he walked out of her life for no apparent reason. I think it was that which made her marry Paolo. And if she found out about it now——' he shrugged '—she might turn against Grandfather and myself. That would really hurt the old man, break his heart. I don't think he could take it—or Francesca either, come to that.'

'But she could,' Elaine said with conviction. 'And she has the right to know. She confided in me a little, and I think she's terribly insecure. That's why she won't let herself fall in love with Sam. You must tell her, Calum.'

'But what about Grandfather?'

'He's a Brodey. He's strong, like you. But I'm sure that Francesca won't take it out on him. She loves him too much.'

He thought for a minute, then nodded. 'All right. I trust your judgement.'

But then Calum was silent for a long moment, and when he spoke again there was bleakness in his voice and his words came out in a harsh stream of confession. 'When I was a great deal younger I had an affair with a married woman—an American. She had a child which she said was mine but which she insisted on passing off as her husband's. I would have accepted the responsibility, of course, but I must admit that I wasn't altogether sorry. The affair was over, and I later felt that she had deliberately let herself get pregnant because her husband wanted children and none had arrived. There were letters about it in the safe. When Tiffany took them I had to go to this woman and tell her that it might all come out.'

Elaine stared at him, bereft of words.

'It wasn't pleasant,' he said shortly, not looking at her. 'Her husband had to be told and I insisted on being with her when she told him. He was, quite naturally, extremely angry. He said that if the story came out he would divorce her. I would then have to acknowledge that the child was mine and take a part in his up-bringing.' With a small, bitter laugh, he went on, 'Just a few weeks ago I told you that you could trust me and now I get involved in this.'

'Why didn't you tell me about it?'

'It was so long ago, so far back in the past, that I had put it out of my mind like a bad dream, almost forgotten about it.'

'Forgotten about a *child*!' she exclaimed, appalled.

Calum looked at her face and stood up, his mouth tightening. 'Unforgivable, I know.' He strode to the door.

'Where are you going?'

'To go on searching for Tiffany. To find out which magazine she sold the article to and try to stop it.' His face white and drawn, he added, 'If you wish to break our engagement, I shall quite understand.' Then he walked out of the flat.

It took a while for Elaine to make the necessary arrangements. There were solicitors to see and schedules to be re-assigned. So it was the end of September before she was able to fly to Oporto again. She hadn't told Calum that she was coming, wasn't even sure that she would find him there in Portugal. When she rang his office in the wine-lodge they told her that he was at the *quinta*, so she immediately hired a car and drove there through the gathering dusk that quickly turned to night.

The *quinta* seemed to be full of activity but she couldn't see any people. There were cars parked everywhere and lights on not only in the house, but in the winery buildings too. Elaine found a space for her car and went to the house, but no one answered her knock and when she went into the unlocked building she found it empty. Mystified, she walked towards the winery and heard the sound of music and singing. The people were all there, crowded into the big room that contained the old grape tanks. Of course, she should have realised; it was the grape harvest.

She pushed her way in, the *quinta* workers good-naturedly making room for her, until she was able to see rows of young people, their arms linked, their skirts and trousers rolled up to their thighs, singing as they trod the huge tank of rich black grapes. In a corner, a man standing on a raised platform was playing an accordion, his red face grinning widely. The place was hot and noisy, everyone laughing, and it looked as if quite a lot of last year's vintage was being drunk to cheer the current one along.

Her eyes swept round the room and at first she didn't see Calum, but then caught sight of him in the shadows behind the accordionist, half turned away from her. Even at that distance she could see the dejection in his shoulders, his bent head.

She gazed at him intently, willing him to turn round, and, as if instinctively aware that he was being watched, he suddenly stepped into the light and saw her. They couldn't reach each other—there were far too many people packing the space between them—but Elaine's heart filled with happiness when she saw the way Calum's face lit up at the sight of her. She tried to tell him with her eyes that she loved him, that she had come to him. But her just being there said it all. The bleakness left his eyes and she could almost see the happiness fill him. The smile, the look of love he gave her then, was one she would treasure all her life.

Calum said something to the accordionist and the man shouted out to everyone that there was food waiting for them in the house. The watchers cheered and gradually made their way out, the grape-treaders cleaning themselves off with towels and following behind.

They waited till everyone had gone and they were quite alone before Calum strode to her and took her in his arms. 'You came! Oh, my darling, you came. I've been praying that you would. My love. My darling. I've missed you so much.'

He showered her mouth with kisses as he spoke and as Elaine was eagerly returning them it was a moment before she could say, 'I've made all the arrangements. I've made Ned and Malcolm my partners. They've taken over and I can stay here for as long as you need me.'

'Oh, my dear. I shall go on needing you for the rest of my life.' He looked down at her. 'But the other thing? The child?'

'We'll do whatever you want to do. Have him live with us, if that's what you want. It doesn't matter. Nothing matters except loving you and wanting to be with you.'

'Oh, my sweet.' He kissed her passionately, and there was deep desire in his eyes when he finally lifted his head. He looked round. 'The house will be full of people.' Then a devilish look came into his eyes. 'Wait.'

Going to the heavy wooden door of the windowless room, he shut it and turned a massive key in the lock. The place was dimly lit—there were only a few light bulbs hanging from the ceiling, making the corners full of shadows. But the atmosphere was warm, still full of laughter and music.

Coming back to her, a light of intense excitement in his eyes, he said urgently, 'Elaine, my roots are in wine. I was brought here to tread these grapes as soon as I could walk. They're in my blood, part of my life. I want them to be as important to you as they are to me.'

She gave a small gasp as she realised what he wanted. But she sensed that this was important to him, sensed also his inner exhilaration. It filled her own mind, and she laughed unsteadily as she said, 'Then I guess we'd better make them part of my life too.'

She didn't know how far he wanted to go, but they undressed each other with eager hands, kissing as they did so, and Calum didn't stop at her outer clothes, taking everything off, so she did the same to him. When they were naked Calum lifted her into his arms and swung her into the wine tank.

The grape juice felt cold at first, making her gasp as it snaked up her legs. It came almost up to her thighs, though not so high on Calum as he joined her. He took the clips from her hair and tossed them aside, bent to kiss her breasts as she arched her neck, her hair soft like fur on her back. The scent of the grapes, their pungent headiness, filled the air, made them drunk with it.

Elaine gave a great sigh of contentment as he went on down, kissing and caressing her. He straightened and scooped up some of the grape juice to smear it over her, doing it slowly, his hands unsteady with excitement, leaving finger trails down her white skin. Trails that he followed with his tongue.

The intoxicating aroma of the grapes and the touch of his hands and mouth were the greatest aphrodisiac Elaine had ever known. She moaned out her rapture, gave little cries of intense pleasure. He straightened, kissed her mouth in ravenous need. Pushing him a little away from her, her eyes dark and sensual, Elaine stooped to fill her hands with juice and do the same to him, doing it slowly, lingeringly, loving every inch of him, feeling him shake with passion beneath her fingertips, beneath the exploring softness of her lips.

Suddenly his desire became uncontrolled. Calum dragged her up and took her mouth with fierce hunger. They swayed together and she felt the grape juice splashing over her, felt his tongue on her skin, her breasts as he licked at her like a man dying of thirst. Their bodies weren't white any longer, were stained red with juice. The flesh of the grapes clung to them, but was greedily eaten, devoured by their mouths as they kissed, shared by their lips.

Then Calum stood back. His mouth was open in a gasping, breathless agony of desire, his body trembling with it. Putting a hand behind her head, the other under her, he bent her back and lowered her into the grapes. Elaine felt the juice rise up her body, the strong scent of the must fill her nostrils, heady as strong wine. It covered her stomach, her breasts, came up to her chin in a ritual baptism that made her as one with him as any marriage vow. He raised her slowly, his eyes devouring her, but filled with so much love.

Dragging her to him, he held her close against his fierce manhood. Held her until she moaned out her own urgent need, her straining hands gripping his shoulders.

'Elaine! Elaine!' Calum cried out her name as he made love to her with passionate eagerness, took her with rapturous abandonment in a place that was a part of his past as she was always to be a part of his present and his future. It was wild, extraordinary, unparalleled, but so was the man she had chosen, and Elaine gave herself with joy and delight, and gloried in the giving.

CHAPTER NINE

ELAINE and Francesca sat together in the garden of the *palácio*. The two women had been there for some time, talking earnestly, confiding the details of their pasts to each other. It was the day after the *barco rabelo* race, the day when, to everyone's amazement, Tiffany had turned up in Oporto. And she had not, it seemed, sold the article she had written after all. The family's private papers were safe and so were their secrets.

They were waiting for Chris to arrive with Tiffany. He had phoned earlier to say that he had found her, that he was going to marry her and that he wanted his future wife treated with respect. 'She's had a bad time in the past,' he told them. 'And she didn't have an abortion: she's still having the baby.'

It was a beautiful day, still hot enough to sit comfortably outside, but the leaves on the trees were starting to turn to gold. The Brodey betrothal ring, a ruby set with diamonds, and almost as old as the House of Brodey, was on Elaine's finger, but, glancing back at the *palácio*, she could still hardly believe that this was to be her home. She loved it already, but it was the *quinta* that would always hold a special place in her heart.

Francesca saw the look in her face and laughed. 'You'll soon get used to it,' she told her. 'And I'm certain you'll be the most wonderful mistress of the Brodey estate.'

'Promise me you'll come and stay as often as you can. Don't let Sam keep you entirely to himself.'

'We've already agreed on that. How about if we extend your business and make it into a transatlantic corporation?'

Elaine's face lit up with eagerness. 'Now *that* is quite an idea.'

They looked at each other and laughed, both supremely happy and content, both looking into the future with excited confidence.

It was at this moment that Chris stepped out of the house with Tiffany at his side. She had a tight grip on his hand and looked uncertainly over at them. Francesca immediately rose and went to meet her.

'Hello, Tiffany. Welcome to the Brodey clan.' She stooped to kiss her on the cheek. 'Come and meet Elaine. Chris, you can go away and find the others. Come back in half an hour,' she ordered imperiously.

Chris hesitated, then grinned. 'Yes, ma'am.'

Taking Tiffany by the hand, Francesca led her over to Elaine, who was standing, waiting. 'This is Elaine Beresford. She and Calum are going to be married.'

Tiffany's eyes widened. 'But you're not——'

'*Blonde*!' both the other girls said together, and burst out laughing.

'I know, isn't it dreadful?' Elaine said, pulling out a chair for Tiffany. 'But Calum doesn't seem to care, and I'm certainly not going to dye it.'

'We've been drinking champagne,' Francesca said as she too sat down. 'But we've got a bottle of mineral water for you, because of the baby. How wonderful that you didn't have an abortion after all. Chris is over the moon.'

Tiffany looked from one to the other of them. 'You don't mind, do you? You really don't mind,' she said in wonder. 'I thought you'd treat me like a leper or something.'

'Chris told us that you'd had a bad time. At the hands of a man, or men, presumably,' Elaine said. 'Well, so have we. We were talking about it just now. We both found it difficult to trust—to love again. To make that leap of faith.' She smiled. 'But I think we've been very lucky, all three of us, because we've each found a man strong enough, and who loves us enough, to conquer our fears and make us whole again.'

Tears came into Tiffany's eyes, and she wiped them away. 'I'm sorry. You're both being very kind,' she said huskily.

'I suppose I ought to go down on my knees and humbly apologise to you,' Francesca said ruefully. 'Sam always said I ought to. I was rotten to you, wasn't I?'

'Yes,' Tiffany agreed, which made them laugh.

'You're so petite!' Francesca exclaimed. 'I was madly jealous. But I'm glad you're going to be my cousin-in-law.'

'I think we ought to drink a toast,' Elaine said. 'Here, let me fill your glasses. Tiffany, do you think you could manage just a sip of champagne? I really think this toast calls for the very best wine.' She filled the glasses and they all raised them. 'Ladies, I give you our future husbands: Chris, Sam and Calum. May they always love us as deeply as they do today.' They clinked their glasses and drank, warmth and happiness in their eyes.

'And here they are,' Francesca announced as she saw the three men come out of the house and walk across the terrace towards them.

'As we will certainly love them,' Tiffany said softly, her eyes on Chris.

Francesca and Elaine looked at her and smiled, then all three of them got to their feet and went to meet the men who'd won their hearts.

MILLS & BOON

CHRISTMAS CRACKERS

*A cracker of a gift pack full of
Mills & Boon goodies. You'll find...*

Passion—in *A Savage Betrayal* by Lynne Graham

A beautiful baby—in *A Baby for Christmas* by Anne McAllister

A Yuletide wedding—in *Yuletide Bride* by Mary Lyons

A Christmas reunion—in *Christmas Angel* by Shannon Waverly

Special Christmas price of 4 books
for £5.99 (usual price £7.96)

Published: November 1995

*Available from WH Smith, John Menzies, Volume One, Forbuoys, Martins,
Tesco, Asda, Safeway and other paperback stockists.*

4 new short romances all wrapped up in 1 sparkling volume.

Join four delightful couples as they journey home for the festive season—and discover the true meaning of Christmas...that love is the best gift of all!

A Man To Live For - Emma Richmond
Yule Tide - Catherine George
Mistletoe Kisses - Lynsey Stevens
Christmas Charade - Kay Gregory

Available: November 1995   **Price: £4.99**

MILLS & BOON

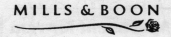

GET 4 BOOKS
AND A MYSTERY GIFT

Return this coupon and we'll send you 4 Mills & Boon Romances and a mystery gift absolutely FREE! We'll even pay the postage and packing for you.

We're making you this offer to introduce you to the benefits of Reader Service: FREE home delivery of brand-new Mills & Boon romances, at least a month before they are available in the shops, FREE gifts and a monthly Newsletter packed with information.

Accepting these FREE books and gift places you under no obligation to buy, you may cancel at any time, even after receiving just your free shipment. Simply complete the coupon below and send it to:

MILLS & BOON READER SERVICE, FREEPOST, CROYDON, SURREY, CR9 3WZ.

No stamp needed

Yes, please send me 4 free Mills & Boon Romances and a mystery gift. I understand that unless you hear from me, I will receive 6 superb new titles every month for just £1.99* each postage and packing free. I am under no obligation to purchase any books and I may cancel or suspend my subscription at any time, but the free books and gifts will be mine to keep in any case. (I am over 18 years of age)

2EP5R

Ms/Mrs/Miss/Mr _____

Address _____

_____

_____ Postcode _____

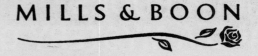

MILLS & BOON

Next Month's Romances

Each month you can choose from a wide variety of romance with Mills & Boon. Below are the new titles to look out for next month.